Called Out

A. G. Mojtabai

NAN A. TALESE

DOUBLEDAY

New York
London
Toronto
Sydney
Auckland

Called Out

MOJTABA

PUBLISHED BY NAN A. TALESE
an imprint of Doubleday
a division of Bantam Doubleday Dell Publishing Group, Inc.
1540 Broadway, New York, New York 10036

DOUBLEDAY is a trademark of Doubleday, a division of
Bantam Doubleday Dell Publishing Group, Inc.

Library of Congress Cataloging-in-Publication Data

Mojtabai, A. G., 1937–
Called out/A.G. Mojtabai.—1st ed.
p. cm.
1. Aircraft accidents—Texas—Fiction. 2. Community life—Texas—
Fiction. I. Title.
PS3563.0374C35   1994
813'.54—dc20   93-32776
CIP

ISBN 0-385-47430-x
Copyright © 1994 by A. G. Mojtabai
All Rights Reserved
Printed in the United States of America
June 1994
First Edition

10 9 8 7 6 5 4 3 2 1

For Genevieve O. Miller,
  Postmaster,
  Dawn, Texas

And to the memory of
  Sammie Parr

Acknowledgment

A LONG-AGO CONVERSATION with a Roman Catholic canon lawyer is situated at the heart of this book. The subject was the sacrament of the anointing of the sick. My questions concerned a disaster situation in which a priest cannot ascertain the religious affiliations of the victims and proceeds to anoint and grant conditional absolution to *all* the dying. I wanted to know what sacrament is effected when the victim anointed happens to be a Muslim or an atheist.

Monsignor James C. Gurzynski's reply was instant and unequivocal. "Wasted oil and a wistful prayer . . ." he said.

His words continued to echo for me during my long labors on this book. If I heard him correctly, it was an answer put forward in the spirit of challenge. Correctly or not, I have taken it as such.

Contents

PART III

"We aren't like a township, old chap. We have no ties of shared experience or blood or memory. In a plane, nobody knows his neighbor. No one belongs to the same Rotary Club or garden society as the person across the aisle. We're just a slice of the history of the world, grievances and all. My old son, this *solidarity* you urge is purest bloody fantasy . . ."

   —Thomas Keneally, *Flying Hero Class*

"Do you see everything at once? My own house is full of things waiting to be seen."

   —Patrick White, *Riders in the Chariot*

ONE

One

First
Witness

THE CLOUDS were thick and moving fast. I'd picked up a weather bulletin some minutes back—I would have kept the radio on in hopes of catching another but I was going through the Fort Worth mixmaster at the time, heart of downtown, trying to keep my mind on the road. Even then, well before rush hour, that was ever a rigorous span. I kept my eyes on the cars ahead, taillights flaring up each time a foot touched a brake; I wasn't the only nervous

driver. The weatherman had said something about precipitation, a percentage of probability, not what kind of precipitation. Could have been anything—rain, sleet, hail—

"All across the top of Texas," I remember him saying.

Minutes before, I'd noticed some flakes of snow flashing
by, testing the air. They were slanting in, salting the windshield. I doubted there'd be any accumulation, though.
The wind was too wild, too scattering, for that.

Yet there were planes crossing overhead, as there always
seemed to be in and around Fort Worth. One about every
three minutes. Military, most likely. I could hear them, I
couldn't see them. I had to assume—I could only hope—
that planes overhead meant that the cloud cover was low.
I've always liked flying—climbing, shedding the earth,
then the cutoff, lifted above confusion, all the little theme
parks of our clusterings laid open to view. But there'd be
nothing to see today.

Soon as I was clear of the city, I loosened my death grip
on the wheel. It wasn't that weather conditions had im-
proved. If anything, the wind seemed to be freshening, the
sky loomed darker, but traffic was easing up. Ordinarily,
I'd set the motor on cruise from here on out and, except
for the last stretch, pretty much let the car take itself
home. Not this time.

Thinking back on it later, the whole day seemed to be
unfolding with a tilt, a relentless downslope towards
something I couldn't yet see but was, all the while, hurry-
ing to meet.

I'd set out for Dallas early, hoping to visit Tom O'Shea,
a classmate from seminary. I'd been feeling restless again.
This happened from time to time. Nothing serious right

yet, but if I ignored it I was afraid the tensions would mount until I'd come to feel my collar was, literally, choking me, an impersonation turned deadly. The mood could be sudden and severe—convulsive. Once, years back, I'd acted upon it and taken leave, but that had led to nothing else. I thought I'd learned a few things since; I'd been monitoring myself, making it my business to talk things over with a friend at the first sign of chafing, the least little lurch of longing. Day before yesterday, I'd called Tom, asking whether he'd be in and arranging a tentative meeting time. Tentative—because I'd promised to look in on the daughter of Martha Gibbon first. As it turned out, my get-together with Tom was doomed; my visit with Jenny Gibbon, futile as it was, lasted longer than expected. Then came the worsening weather.

Martha—Jenny's mother—I didn't know well. She'd moved from Hardesty to Bounds back in early summer, but the first time she showed up in church was in February, wanting her throat blessed at the feast of St. Blaise. Her daughter had run away from home two years back; that was before the mother came to town, so I'd never set eyes on the girl. My assignment was to see if I couldn't persuade her to come back, or at least to start her talking. No one else in the family had been able to get through to her. Same old story: the parents come to me as a last resort. It's always way too late. I didn't promise anything, though I told Martha I'd give it a try.

"Oh, another thing," Martha added, as if in afterthought. "Jenny was pregnant when she ran away. And she kept the child. He's with her at the shelter now."

It was hopeless from the start. "I don't know you" were

the first words out of Jenny's mouth. I've never been comfortable with teenagers anyway, barely surviving that phase in my own life. Add to that the single motherhood factor—Mary notwithstanding—and I was already way out of my depth. I jangled the change in my pocket and hoped the visit would go quickly.

Eighteen years old, but she looked years younger, not much more than a child, herself—sullen, defiant, scared. We set out for a nearby cafeteria. She straddled the infant on her hip, then settled him on her lap while I went through the line for the three of us. I chose rice pudding for the baby. He was old enough to dabble in it with spoon, fingers and fist, making a real mess of himself in the process, and a lot of noise. *Shaped* noise—not words, but almost, well along. When whatever it was he was trying to say failed to communicate, he'd start to scream with frustration. Then Jenny would slap him around a little and call him stupid. "You shouldn't call him that," I said. "His name isn't really 'Stupid,' is it?"

"Why not!" she was quick to reply. "He acts stupid. And, anyhow, he doesn't know the difference. He's too young to know what it means."

"What's his real name?"

"Sam—why? What's it to you, Mister?" A string of abusive four-letter words followed. It was a performance calculated to shock—I'd been through this kind of thing before. What do they think? Where do they think we've been all our lives? That we've simply fallen out of the trees to earth? I'd heard those words often enough—I knew them. They had no shock value left. I waited in silence for her to finish.

A social worker at the shelter had filled me in on Jenny's history before I'd been allowed to meet her. Three months pregnant, she'd hitched a ride from Hardesty. Detoured off in some of the bigger towns like Abilene, making her way, eventually, down to Fort Worth. In her many months of wandering, she never got farther than Tarrant County. That's pitifully close if your aim is to see the world. She'd made a little vertical progress, briefly, moving up from Wendy's to a fancy stockyard cafe in Fort Worth, until her pregnancy began to slow her down. Then she'd found a protector—what looked like a protector—a man old enough to be her father. He'd set her up in a small apartment on the outskirts of the city. When she started to get restless again, he turned her out into the streets. But not without beating up on her first. Finally, she'd come to this shelter. She was restless here, too, but unwilling to go back to high school and finish up, or to make any sustained effort towards learning a marketable skill. Anybody could see the turmoil: fingernails gnawed to the quick, her forehead and cheeks blotchy with angry spots no makeup could hide. She never looked me in the face; it was all sly, sidling glances, quick left to right and back, over me and past. Sam, on the other hand, persisted in giving me a full frontal stare. His eyes seemed all pupil. He had a brooding look, deeply serious, taking my measure.

Then, all of a sudden, he reached for me with moist fingers, seized hold of my thumb and locked onto it. He tugged with unexpected strength, I tugged back, a conversation of sorts—and one of those zigzags I have to watch out for. *In another life* . . . is how it begins. One of those moments. My pull—your pull, back and forth, we rocked with it; I was captive—captivated; the baby crooned, his mouth glistening with smiles. I don't know how long we might have gone on with this had Jenny not interrupted, "Boy, time sure flies when you're having fun!"—jolting him back to herself. Sam yelped once, then dropped me; the game was over. My face flooded with heat, even my ears—I embarrass easily. And I'd come, after all, on business. So I launched into it: "Your mother asked me to see you. She could help you out with Sam— she's eager to. Why not give her a chance? She misses you. Come home."

"To Bounds?" She paused, as if actually giving it a moment's thought. "To Bounds?"—laughing now—"No way! Dullsville, you mean? Besides, you forget, I never lived there."

All the while I was saying it, I remember thinking: it's poetic justice I'm the one who's been asked to call her back, when here I've been wanting to leave, myself. Wanting to leave Bounds or my role in it—I couldn't tell which, and assumed I was boxed in by both. After I'd delivered my prepared speech, I tried the gifts I'd brought along—a woman's magazine, a tin of brownies, a note from her younger sister. A cardigan, gift-wrapped. She trashed the wrapping, making a loose, crumpled ball of it. Sam batted the thing with his fists while Jenny examined the sweater at arm's length, refolding it carefully, without bothering to try it on.

Adolescence! Supposed to be the best years of our lives. Did nobody recall how it really was? The misery, sheer misery of it? Jenny brought the mess of mine back to me. The boorishness: anger overspilling at the slightest touch, the fractured dreams, my skin boiling up. Voice breaking, unpredictable from one moment to the next. A bunch of us getting together in an abandoned shed to compare our "equipment." Humiliating, but I passed. But it was no relief. Images coming to me unbidden, dredged up from darkness. Sins of impurity—radiant. Searing. Confessing and falling again. Confessing with firm purpose of amendment, and falling again—

"How long you been in Bounds?" Jenny asked on our way back. "Going on six years," I told her. "And you ask me why I'm not coming back," she said. "If you don't know, Mister, I can't tell you."

I hadn't worn my collar. My day off, for one thing; for another, the more I thought about meeting Jenny the more I suspected the collar would prove a handicap. It would be a trade-off, I figured; what I lost in the way of authority, I'd gain in humanity. I'd misfigured, badly. That was a deliberate, calculated "Mister" she called me, loaded with venom. And she did it two or three times. I'd introduced myself as "Father Mark," and I realized she was flirting with me when she said with a kind of leer, a certain slide of tongue over lip, "I don't believe you're really a priest."

Some believe it, some don't. I shrugged. Didn't bother to answer Jenny. I've questioned it myself, often enough. Yet it wasn't by accident that I'd become a priest. Not the best of reasons maybe. I'd backed into it somehow, fleeing and seeking. *Still*—it wasn't by accident. I'd been called to it. Summoned. There was a voice, my own. And one word. I could feel the air clench in my throat, though nobody else heard it. The word was: *No*. But God never spoke to me about what He wanted me to do. Not a word, not a whisper.

Nobody pushed me into the Church. Day like today, I had to keep reminding myself of that fact. Dad was sitting at the dining room table playing solitaire when I announced my intention of going to seminary. I could still see his hands deftly shelling out cards, not missing a beat, all the while I was speaking. That's the image that stays with me—his hands, nothing of his face. Then there was only the rapid patter of cards, the heavy beating of my heart. At last he spoke: "So you won't be bringing any money in." His business, a repair shop for small machines, wasn't doing well; he could have used a contribution from me. "Have you spoken to your mother about this?" he asked. I had. Mom said simply, "If that's what you really want." She was far from overjoyed, I knew, for this meant that I wouldn't be marrying and filling the house with grandchildren. There was only me—an only child.

I couldn't blame my parents for being puzzled; nothing had prepared them for my taking such a step. As a tot, I'd never played priest-at-the-altar with my little friends, as so many of the other seminarians had. My wish list had been the same as any other boy's growing up in West Texas. What I wanted most was to own a hunting knife; once I had the knife, I wanted a gun. It came, finally, on my fourteenth birthday: a Stevens single shot .22 caliber rifle; I doted on it, cleaning the barrel and oiling the stock over and over. I shot a few rabbits with it, then wounded a cat and had to put the creature out of his misery. Then I lost all interest in guns.

I'd turned fifteen and it was happening to me—whatever happens when you turn that corner. I'd learned to social dance the spring before, fox-trot, I remember, I forget what else. *Slide, slide, clomp, clomp, slide* and supposed to be graceful. It was all an agony of embarrassment for me. I couldn't look girls in the eyes, couldn't imagine what in the world to say to them. I overheard my mother telling one of my aunts, "Mark is going through a phase." I didn't like that at all—the idea of my going through predictable phases, as if the course of my life had been charted in advance. A generic life—not mine, not willed, not shaped. Not chosen.

"To *Bounds?*" Jenny had stared, her eyes wide with astonishment, when I asked her whether she wouldn't consider coming back. I wanted to let her know that I, too, swore at her age never to return to my hometown, to leave and never look back, but she never gave me a chance. The story is familiar enough, happens in all these little towns; it's the young and the old, the moving and the fixed. See it all the time.

The place I grew up in was a lot like Bounds. Typical High Plains town. Named Windy—and for good reason. One minute you'd see wheatfields ripening peacefully in the sun, seized in the next by wind, dust, flash flood, hail. There wasn't a whole lot going on except for the wind, the beating sun, the blowing dust. Wind and weather, weather and wind. A sea of grass as far as the eye could reach—

Strange the way that spaciousness began to draw in . . . It was after I'd had my gun for a while. October—I was fifteen. Up to then, I'd loved the place, had grown up one with it. West Texas grit and grind, tough and proud of it—that was the tradition. Life had been hard in Windy from the start. It wasn't written in our catechism, but it was taught along with it, how the first Catholic settlers celebrated Palm Sunday using bear grass for palms. Things grew a little more comfortable after that. Then came the dust bowl days they loved to tell about, people barely scratching along, then recovery and almost comfortable once again. Then depressed. That year when things turned round for me was hard for everyone in Windy. The harvest was poor that fall; worse was on the way. But we didn't know that yet and looked forward to the annual Oktoberfest, same as every year.

I'd always enjoyed the spectacle of it, our one real mixer. Everybody came, from the mayor on down, even the derelicts from the Calvary Mission shelter. And there were three other drifters who showed up that year; they weren't affiliated with Calvary, or anything. I saw one of the young mothers aiming a finger in their direction: a perfect example, I suppose, of what children who didn't eat, wash, or obey properly, grew up to be. "You see what I'm seeing?" she said. "Take a good look." They were living scarecrows, with gap-toothed smiles, grizzle, matted hair, stinking clothes. Young men, but they seemed ancient, already earth-bent from scavenging.

They'd started out at the back of the tent, draining beer dregs and abandoned pop bottles, pocketing chunks of pretzel, raking the trash bins for cigarette butts. They inched forward to watch the German dancers, moving front and center for the Vienna waltzers, and staying put for the rest of the display—the Polish dancers, then the Mexican dancers. I overheard them talking: it was all "polka" to them; they loved it, all of it.

When the call came, as it always did, for the chicken dance, nearly everybody joined in. All ages and sizes. It would go on and on for fifteen, twenty minutes, speeding up as it went. "Waggle, waggle," the caller would sing out. And they'd flap their fledgling wings (arms folded at the elbows, hands in armpits), then "quack, quack" and "wiggle, wiggle," and they'd flutter their tail feathers (smiling lasciviously, shaking their bottoms). Then they'd start circling—two circles, inner and outer. Whenever the music stopped, the dancers froze, and the person facing each of them—man, woman, or child, whoever it chanced to be—was the new partner. And then—with a "swing your partner round and round"—the music would strike up again.

As soon as those scarecrows entered the circle, that chicken dance began to look like nothing so much as a dance of death. They swung their partners hard to their own fast, jagged rhythms—nothing to do with the music. You'd see their partners arcing their backs away from them, straining away, yet helpless, reeling, cinched at the waist. One of the drifters had coupled up with a kid. She was maybe six years old and he was giving her a twirl, a wild ride, her feet dangling inches from the floor. I could still see her face: a tiny fright mask with tight mouth, and wide, glittering eyes.

When the music ended, the three scarecrows retreated to the edge of the tent, back to their cadging for butts and beer, and some of us—the spectators, at least—we missed them. They'd been a diversion.

Members of the band were starting to pack up with many a phony "auf wiedersehn" and "ach zo!" They were a bunch of rednecks just like us, even though they'd come all the way from East Texas. Oktoberfests were their specialty.

The master of ceremonies was doing her frantic best to distract us from the fact that the band was getting ready to leave. Anything to hold the crowd together. In her Tyrolean cap with its red feather, peasant blouse and skirt, embroidered apron, and clogs, she, too, was acting a part. In real life, I knew her as Mrs. Owens, a local farmer's wife, who, far as I knew, had spent all her days in Windy. Maybe she had a German grandmother or great-aunt or something. Nobody could fault her for effort. She dreamed up one distraction after another: a Swiss watch was auctioned off, a pair of wooden clogs, a pitcher of beer. Then she started a beauty contest for the men—roll up your trousers if you thought you had a good leg and come on up to the dance floor. Four came, all young, but not a looker in the lot: fat, lean as a rail, bulging with calf, yet-to-be-seen—there was one of each. The one still covered up was wearing long johns and boots and having a time of it. "How about it?" Mrs. Owens urged. "Show us some leg!" He did, finally, but it was hardly worth waiting for.

Then one of the scarecrows threw himself into the ring. He became number five. Mrs. Owens challenged him to show us some leg. He did, and we all clapped. "Why don't you tie some knots in those legs and give us some knees!" she taunted. He did that too—rolled up his jeans to mid-thigh and crooked his stick legs to give us some knees. I hooted and clapped as he did so. It looked like a real comedy shaping up, live and unrehearsed, and nobody knew where it would lead. Prancing, lifting his knees high, the man was playing to the crowd. He shifted to bumping and grinding across the dance floor, elbows flapping—shades of the chicken dance. Then gave us a burlesque of a Vienna waltz, a belly dance, an Irish jig. He was plastered, shameless—we loved it. I hollered along with everybody else, laughing so hard I could taste it. Water streamed from my eyes.

No question who the winner was. Only then did Mrs. Owens ask for his name. He told her it was Billie. "Billie!" we echoed, delighted to hear it, and we hooted and hollered some more. The prize was an oversized T-shirt with some beer company logo emblazoned across it. Billie grabbed it and, waving it high overhead, started to dance with it—a stripper's dance. Off with the old shirt!—he twirled it round one finger. We cheered as he bared his chest, so shallow you could count the staves of his rib cage.

I was laughing hard as anyone when the air backed up in my throat. The word was *No*—I nearly choked on it. Suddenly Mrs. Owens was trying to push Billie offstage. She meant business. Not a trace of her former smile. She gave a high sign to one of the sheriff's men standing in our midst—I guess because she thought Billie's disrobing act might not end at the waist. And because there were children watching. The officer lost no time in trundling Billie off. The crowd began to trickle away. It was no longer amusing. Only after I left did I begin to wonder why it had ever seemed amusing.

That was in the fall, the first *No*. I didn't dwell on it. The season passed. Soon after, the cold closed in. Even in

winter, you'd still see men standing on the sides of the
road, carrying signs that said WORK FOR FOOD. Spring came
—no better. Came summer, one of the driest on record.
Oil, gas, cattle, wheat, and milo (we called it "maize"
back then) were what we depended on, and oil was down,
gas was down, rainfall not even a rumor. Tumbleweed
piled up on our porchfronts, a fire hazard. The mayor
recommended we burn it before it burned us. Most of our
lawns were bleached out—there was water rationing in
town.

Fifteen going on sixteen!—that dry, desolate summer.
Why did I think of it then as my last summer? I still do.
That going-on-sixteen summer was the last of something,
childhood's end, fateful. I was restless as the wind. Maybe
it was the pain of being stretched out too quickly, too
tight in every bone and tendon. I'd grown tall and weedy
—six foot one and still shooting up. Seemed like the
stretching would never stop.

Days, I'd be working at Dad's shop. Evenings and days-
off, I spent riding my bike around town, going nowhere,
just riding. I didn't own a car yet—didn't expect to for
years to come. Les Miller, my best friend up to then, had
taken over his older brother's car. It was low and sleek.
Ben Honea had a jeep he'd worked two jobs to save up
for. He'd painted it electric blue and boosted it high above
the wheels, so you couldn't miss it coming down the road.
Low riders, high riders, it was all the same—all pointless
—to me. The dream then was of owning a pickup with a
rifle rack and a couple of guns to hang on the rack. Then
roving along with a girl, well stacked, in shorts and halter,
on the seat beside. That summer, most of the girls were

wearing halters without straps, so the big item of discussion was what, if anything, the girl was wearing underneath, and how to find out. Ben and Les would talk about girls' halters and calf cuttings with the same half-murderous rasp of excitement. The pickup truck, the rifle rack, and the girl had almost been my dream, too, but, for some reason, when the moment came, I never launched onto them. I'd missed a step, someway.

Instead, I'd spend my free time by myself, riding my bike around. Setting out, I'd cast a backward glance at the driveway hoop where I'd spent the summer before shooting baskets—overhand, underhand, hooks, spin-and-drives, endlessly, compulsively, getting better and better at it. As if any of it mattered.

I hadn't touched a basketball in months. I rode my bike in circles, from one end of town to the other, round and round, as though I were caught in a maze and well and truly lost. Downtown after banking hours, there'd be only a few remaining cars and pickups parked with their noses snub up to the curb, ranged along it like cattle at a long feed trough. But the cars were fewer and the trough emptier than it had ever been before.

Usually, I'd stop in at the library. I didn't so much read as *eat* books in those days. And I wasn't particular: I'd read through almost anything I'd started. It was an escape for me.

That summer, even the library reading room was a mirror of our woes. It looked like a bus depot, full of passengers who'd been stalled for one reason or another. But these people were going nowhere. Farm and ranch hands, pipe-welders, roughnecks from the oil crews, vagrants—

they'd taken over most of the soft browsing chairs and the tables closest to the electric fans. Most of them were fugitives from Calvary Mission across the street; they'd sung for their supper at the afternoon service but, once fed, weren't about to get themselves conscripted for the evening service. The librarian had posted a new set of rules in the foyer, a long list of prohibitions: *no soliciting, no loitering, no sleeping, no staring, no touching*—

No staring—

It was a mean summer in more ways than one.

After the library, I'd pedal slowly back home, circling our church at least once, nearing it, and veering away. When I was tired of circling, I'd head for home.

We had a boarder living with us at the time—Dan Hawkins, a retired blacksmith and welder, who'd owned the shop my father had taken over and converted to small machine repairs. Mr. Hawkins hankered after large machines, the hand-tooled kind. Coming into the house, I'd hear him going at it—his theme song about the good old days of drag farming, of steel lug tractors, one-way discs and lister shares, golden days before the state and federal men walked the turnrows sniffing for herbicide residues. He was stuck on the old ways, and his talk was all has-beens, bygones, betternots—all stifling. "Spittingly boring," I called it. I minced no words back then.

When Mr. Hawkins wasn't holding forth, we ate in silence, a silence broken only by the clashing of forks and knives and the single question my father asked at least once a day: "How long can this keep up?" He meant the heat and the drouth, but I took it as a none too subtle reference to my ceaseless roaming and said nothing in reply.

The evening of the day it happened—the day that changed everything for me—I ate quickly, then took off. I had plans, for once, and was already late. I was going to meet the old gang—Les Miller, Ben Honea, Pete Graff, and Tom White. Why, all of a sudden, after steering clear of them for weeks? I wanted to try and make amends, I guess. Or, if that didn't work out, to remind myself why I'd been keeping away. They usually gathered at Simmons's field before dark. The field had been ours to roam for a number of years, ever since Mrs. Simmons had retired to a nursing home. There was a small playa lake in the middle of it, where we used to splash around and cool our heels. I expected the playa would be dry, or almost, that summer, but still hoped there'd be a dab of water when I got there, enough to rinse the sweat from my face at least.

There were two different stories about the playa: one, that it was an ancient buffalo wallow; another, that it was a depleted natural gas sump. Depending on which you believed, you were typed as romantic or practical. I'd always opted for the buffaloes.

Something else on Simmons's field had always excited our curiosity—an old Burlington Northern boxcar, ancient and rusted, a leaning thing. Most of the time, we avoided getting right up to it for fear it would fall on us, but every now and then, we'd hear stirrings and knew there was somebody taking shelter there. The latest was a deaf-mute, feeble-minded, or maybe out of her mind. Nobody knew where she'd come from, or when exactly. I'd caught my first glimpse of her back in April. Les had named her "Rosie" because her hair had red lights in it. She had the palest skin, unnaturally white. Impossible to tell her age; we never got that close.

I hid my bike in a tangle of weeds near the fence. Everywhere I looked, Johnsongrass was taking over, crowding the banks of the road, obliterating the bar ditches, standing nearly as tall as I was. And everything else dry as a bone. There was a saying in our part of the country that certain things were as hard to kill off as Baptists and Johnsongrass. They were fierce, both of them—unstoppable.

I spread the wires and climbed through the fence. The field was full of ancient milo stalks they'd forgotten to plow under; they sliced at my shins as I passed. The playa was in a deep depression, but the land sloped gradually down to it, so I paid little mind to my descent.

Nobody around, except for some small rustlings underfoot. I was way too late.

Then, coming closer, I wasn't sure. I could see grass churning ahead. I heard, thought I heard, wings thrashing. I blinked: made out some clumped shape crouched at the edge of the playa. The sun was level with my eyes, I remember. The animal was large. I moved forward quietly as I could.

It was no animal, of course. I knew who it was.

It was pretty strange . . . Here I was, decades later, driving through deepening fog and wind, minding the few traffic signs, paying reasonable attention to the gasoline truck bearing down upon me from the rear, and trying not to swerve for thinking of her. Of Rosie. I kept seeing her, sharper, more real than the truck overtaking me, etched as indelibly in my mind's eye as if I'd been staring straight at the sun. She climbed to her feet; I came no closer. I remember nothing in sequence after that. Only the blackness of her open mouth in the whiteness of her face. A sound came from the blackness—a bleat. Lambs bleat like that. I must have made some motion, wanting to disappear, to evaporate on the spot. She fell to a crouch again, turned and crawled back to the boxcar. I never saw anything human crawl that fast.

I knew what had happened. Her face was scratched, her blouse torn—one breast exposed. I knew what had gone on as surely as if I'd been part of it.

I'd never seen a breast before.

I could never think of it again without remembering how it felt to claw my way up out of that playa, that sinkhole. The rest of that week, month, however long it took, was featureless—eventless. Next thing I knew, I was staring at a door, St. John's rectory, summoning up my courage to knock, then old Mrs. Williams, the housekeeper, waving me on into the foyer. Father Fogarty was hard of hearing, so I couldn't help knowing what she said.

"Young man to see you," she began.

"Is he a gentleman?" Father Fogarty asked.

"He's much too young to tell, Father."

"Guess you better show him in." He sounded none too delighted.

Father Fogarty was settled in an easy chair, reading the evening paper, when I entered. In his civvies and house-slippers he looked quite domesticated—much like my father might ten years down the road. His living room was a fussy one with large, heavily padded armchairs, covered in dark flocked velvet. Tatting like cobwebs—those lace doilies that ladies liked—all over the place, defending each spot that flesh or hair might touch.

"So . . ." Father Fogarty greeted me. He sighed, as I recalled, folded up the paper carefully, centering it on his lap. "So what can I do for you?" he asked. Like any shop-keeper.

I'd rehearsed this scene before knocking but, when the crunch came, forgot all my lines. I still can't recall how I broke the silence, what the first words were. Just a total blank there. He told me to sit down. I did. He leaned forward. "Let me make sure I heard you right," he spoke slowly. "You want to be a Trappist, that correct?" I nod-ded. "Where'd you ever come by such a notion?"

I don't know what I said. It was a wild guess, a stab in the dark. I'd read a book. Merton, I suppose. It had some-thing, not a little, to do with the utter predictability of my parents' conversations and with Dan Hawkins's intermi-nable monologues. I wanted silence—not empty silence, not the wounded silence that sometimes fell over our din-ner table like a pall, but perfected silence. Silence, or psalms.

"When I was your age, I wanted to join the circus," Father Fogarty said. "First things first." His eyes were small with laughing. "Before you run off and join the Trappists, do you mind telling me what makes you think you have a calling to the religious life?"

I stared at the floor; I had no good answer to that. I'd made, at best, a lurch towards something, delivered myself over. "I came to you to find out" was the most I could say.

"We will," he said, completely serious now.

When I thought of all the miles I'd put in, cycling around town—all that circling! At another time, in another place, I might have dropped out of school and hit the open road, built a tree house, or boarded ship. I might —I might have—but I hadn't—and now, up ahead—

BOUNDS—60 MILES. The first sign for it.

Nearing the homestretch. That's when I tend to grow careless. Back to the present: I needed my wits about me. I fiddled with the radio dial, caught the tail end of the news —the financial report. The prime was up; the dollar was down against the yen; a certain brand of hardware beat the competition cold. I waited for a weather report. Wheat and cattle prices. The cattle trade was closing on a very slow note. I didn't like what I was seeing. The fog seemed to be thickening, or maybe I was moving deeper into the thick of it. No precipitation, but I had to gear down to second and hold tight to the wheel again to keep from veering. The wind had a mind of its own, or, rather, several minds—that was the problem. Still no weather report. Futures, instead: sorghum, soybeans. An ad for an antibiotic against shipping fever and blackleg.

Futures continued: milo, oats, spot silver, crude oil, a steady stream of numbers trickling into my ears, then something *poured*—the opening trumpet strains of the "Welcome to Glory" show. The sky was bleak, soot-colored, far from glorious. They must have given the weather earlier—I'd missed it.

"Joy Unspeakable" was the first hymn. I cracked open the window a few turns and took a taste of the air. Half a minute told me all I wanted to know, nothing I didn't already know. *Head home—Get there—fast—*

Easier said than done, of course. I still had a stretch of country road to go. "Welcome to Glory" paused for an announcement. Aha! Small bells chiming—then a siren. "Severe thunderstorm watch, possible hail, deadly lightning . . ." A travel advisory: "If you don't have to travel, don't," the weatherman said. "Sit back and stay in Clemence County."

The Glory Hour resumed. It was "message time" with Pastor Mort Willigis, of what church I didn't catch. Lutheran, I guessed, Missouri Synod, something of that stripe. "You can't work your way to salvation," he proclaimed, "no way you can earn it!" Lutheran, yes, still hammering away at works and indulgences . . . "All our righteousness is filthy rags"—he sounded quite pleased about it. There followed chapter and verse.

Why listen? To keep abreast of the competition, I suppose. I'm still curious about what's out there. Besides—I needed some voice outside me, even if I wasn't entirely attending to it, simply to keep me from drifting off. Country music or easy listening never kept my attention for long. The biggest challenge on this last leg of the journey is keeping awake. Sometimes it's fifteen, twenty minutes or more between cars—not a sign of human life except for a few pump jacks nodding, mile upon mile of wire fence and scattered clumps of cattle grazing behind the wire. Every now and then I'd spot a coyote lashed to a fence post, nose-diving—looks like he's flying into the ground— his tail looped back over his spine. Signifying what? Scarecrow? Totem? Trophy? I've seen this all my life but never have been able to figure it. I heard Willigis saying, "Paul is lifted from prison, the paralytic from his bed, the young man from his tomb, yet the prison, the bed, and the tomb remain . . ."

Just amazing . . . how the mind strays. I never did take in how Pastor Willigis wrapped it all up—the prison, the tomb, the filthy rags—nor anything much else of what followed the Glory Hour beyond a welcome battering of noise. Could half an hour have passed? I was moving along pretty slowly, still in second, struggling with diminishing visibility and the buffeting of the wind. It had been a long drive and it wasn't over. A long, fruitless day. I'd done nothing for Jenny. I pressed on, ticking off a list of what needed doing the next day, making a mental note to add the girl's name to my Mass intentions.

BOUNDS—24 MILES

Look sharp.

I seemed to have lost my radio reception. I fiddled with the dial again but only got a few blurts of static. It was just then, anyway, that I noticed something overhead. It wasn't alarming at first. Strange maybe, but—

I stared at it for what must have been a mile or more. One of those long jets with sleeked-back wings, the engines rear-mounted. Nothing out of the ordinary in that, but it seemed suspended, making no forward progress, only rocking a little in the air. And it was way too close to the ground. So close, you could see the little porthole windows. You could even count them if you wanted to.

Took my breath away for a moment there. For a split second, I even thought of taking cover—as if anybody could.

Caught myself whispering, "Help them!"—too shocked to even cross myself, when the plane yawed to one side, recovered, and lifted straight up, as if a string had been pulled on high. Higher and smaller, until the red light on the underbelly of the fuselage was no more than a spark. Then the whole thing vanished, making me wonder whether I'd seen it or dreamt it.

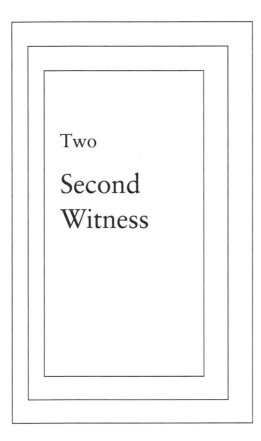

Two

Second Witness

I WAS ABOUT to call it a day. We close up at two at the post office here in Bounds. We'd had no phone and no lights for the past hour or so. The wind must of taken down a power line. My heater's electric, too, so I'd been wearing my coat indoors.

My weather vane, my little right finger—the one that's cocked—had been achy and swollen from the start. Steady blowing, the sun in and out. Then—out, the sky lowering.

The cold seeped in. And something else, I felt it, like coming close to a power station or a great big tuning fork, something thrumming in the air, hearing it not in my ears, but up and down my whole skin, churning all around me. Then a little click—I'm pretty well sure that's what the sound was—and the power died.

I didn't mind the fact that I was closing the day with no customers. It was a respite, really. Everybody'd been acting a little crazy. The kind of crazy where people keep asking, "How long can winter last? Can I stand it one day longer?" Keep forgetting how it's like this every year round about now. What did they use to call this time— crocuses coming up, frost chilling them down, everything cracked with cold, spring and income tax on their way, right around the corner? Eyefuls? Idles? . . . Hides? Something. Ides! Ides of March is what. That's where we were, in the wild middle of March.

The office looked shipshape, as tidy as ever you'd find it. No unfinished business, far as I could see. Closing up was all, fixing the postmark stamp, tweezing out the old day and squeezing in the new. I do that last, usually, after putting out the mailbags and tending to the flag and such.

Most of my work was finished now, and not only at the post office, I realized. What with the kids grown and married and settled all over the state. Nothing more to do there. Except for Rob's baptism, which nagged at me every now and then. I disliked mentioning it, but last night I couldn't hold it in any longer.

Rob's the new grandbaby, Al and Mary's. They've only got the one child. Al's *my* baby, my youngest. Only saw Rob once: he was a bare month old, but already the image of his grandad—the *image!* Troy never lived to see him, but I guess he would of figured that, someday, one of his grandkids or great-grandkids or great-greats would take after him. Sooner or later all things come round. It's too bad they live way down in Corpus Christi—grandkids sure do spice up our later lives. I'd see them again in June —I had a whole two weeks coming to me in June, but the days really yawned out till then.

Just couldn't hold myself back when I called Al last night. "Dreamed about your father, couple nights ago," I said. "In my dream— Are you listening, Al?" Something told me he wasn't. "I'm fine, Ma," he said, so I *knew* he wasn't. There wasn't any stopping me then. "Al, this is important. Now listen, you hear! In the dream I had, your father told me we were all 'licensed and insured'—except for Rob." Al was listening then. "What the hell is that supposed to mean?" he asked. "What else could it mean but baptized?" I said. "Your father's worried about Rob's baptism." Al was listening hard then. I could tell because his foot was waggling with impatience; I could hear him clearly, toe-tapping on the waxed wood floor in Corpus Christi all the way to Bounds. Al and Mary don't have rugs—it's the fashion in their circle not to, to buff up the old wood instead. None of my business, I know, but when I think of all the years Troy and I had to wait, saving up for our first rug! And Al and Mary have the money for it . . . But it's none of my business.

I didn't mean to nag. Which is why I didn't mention how long it'd been since I'd last gotten a letter. "Write when you can someday," I say. Well, of course, kids don't write letters anymore. It's all phone and fax, drive-in, fast food, what-have-you—not one minute to spare. Those answering machines, now! Al's got one, too. I always leave the same message: "Hello, machine. I'm calling to speak to somebody live." But my brand of humor seems to be out of date, along with everything else.

Al's the baby of the family, the last to leave home and, of course, one part of me didn't want him to leave. Not ever. I admit I favored him, spoiled him maybe a little bit. The point is—I know his every mood, I knew full well what was coming. "You're chewing on me again, Ma," he said. "I told you, me and Mary are tending to it. We mean to do it. Soon as we find the right place." They've been shopping around for the right church for I don't know how long—it's always something. I mentioned that.

"Ma, this is just ridiculous!" Al said.

"It isn't to me," I said, "nor to your father."

I admit it was kind of a peculiar dream, because Troy wouldn't of minded one way or the other. Except for my pushing him, he never was a churchgoing man.

Another thing about that dream I hadn't mentioned to Al: Troy had passed on some personal advice to me. "You oughta travel," he said. "*Now*—while you're still able to." I couldn't see Troy speaking in the dream, no face behind the words, no lips moving, but there'd been no mistaking his voice—gravelly and slow. He said more: "The days are soon coming when dizziness powders your head." I patted my hair. In the dream, I could see myself from the outside: my hair bled white, all white.

For a fact, though, the gray's only threaded in. Coming along, but there's still some color left. One more day like today, though, and I'd be solid white forthwith. It had been a day of solid pettiness, with the power blackout coming on top of it, and here I was sitting in my coat indoors, chilled through and through, feeling sorry for myself. I do have arthritis pretty bad in my hands, hip, and knees; the damp doesn't help.

And—I'd been hours standing and taking it. Nobody liked the new stamps, the ones with the rock stars on them. And they didn't want to use the old LOVE stamps for paying bills. They'd never taken to twenty-nine cents for first-class postage to start with. Too complicated is the complaint on that. It's more trouble for me than for them, so I always ask: "Would you rather pay out a penny more and round it off even?" No, they wouldn't. *Well,* then? I tell you what! You'd of thought the U.S. Postal Service had declared it National Complaints Day. Wayne Hollis didn't like the new linoleum—Joy Major did. If you don't like the color, look elsewhere, I say. Add to that, some of the old folk taking the occasion to fret about their new postboxes being too high or too low—we'd gotten key boxes finally, but nobody stopped to appreciate that.

It only takes three or four to start a fuss and the rest all chime in and nobody knows where it began or how to end it. I'd reassigned the postboxes after the renovations. By lot—I thought that would be fairest. Way it turned out, some had to stoop and some had to stretch up, while a few others had it easy at arm's level. That was the luck of the draw. I was ready to do some swapping for real hardship, like Geneva Wilson's arthritis, or Carla Simms's varicose veins, but most of the fuss was just scrapping, petty, plain and simple.

Why *not* get away for a while? Sitting there in that ashy

gray light, I kept coming round to my dream and back into that conversation with Troy. It was true that we'd saved up over the years. I could go to Palm Beach or L.A. or New York City, cities I'd never seen. But I wasn't eager to. I'd never hungered for the new and strange—not in foods, people or places. First time I ate Mexican, I flashed hot and cold all night long. Who needs it? Now I'd gotten used to it and liked my hot sauce *el scorcho,* but who needed it to start with? Stick with what you know, I say. With *who* you know. Strangers are more so east of the Mississippi, I've been told. I really wasn't eager to budge from Bounds, vexing as people here can be. I was more ready to wrap my house around me and go on inside forever, if the truth be known.

It was one of my "hello, Nothing" moods coming on—I recognized it. The weather wasn't helping, of course. I knew they would pass, mood and weather together, in a day or two. What I needed was a hot cup of tea to perk me up, and a bite of something. And to rest my feet. Day like today, retirement sure looked tempting. Problem was, the minute I retired, the government might take the opportunity to shut us down; we're only a fourth-class post office, after all. Call it cost-cutting or streamlining, and force everybody in Bounds to travel miles up the road to the county seat in Hardesty to pick up their mail. So that was my worry there.

It was going on two—close to it. Just a couple of things to do before calling it a day.

Outside, it was hard to keep upstanding, no exaggeration. I commenced taking down the flag, wondering whether I'd have to give up and leave it to be blown to shreds out in the weather, but then came a moment's slack, and I hauled, mightily, bundling it in the crook of my arm, quick as it came. The flag's supposed to go up briskly and down slowly. Mostly I try—and *do*—but, right then, I'd defy anybody to.

It was then that I heard something toiling overhead. I glanced up: a big jet. It was hanging there—not going anyplace—just hanging there in some sort of stall. Then it started to shake—its tail only a flutter, but its nose dipping and rising in a wobble, like nose and tail were dealing with different kinds of weather.

We're not on anybody's overflight path, so we tend not to see a whole lot of traffic up there. Most of the time, it's nothing but crop dusters. Piloting a crop duster's not too bright of a future from what I've heard. Nobody wants to insure them—they fly too low and flirt with too many power lines. Anyway, it was flying too high for a crop duster, but way too low for a big jet the size it seemed to be. I puzzled over it, little bit, then ducked back inside. Right quick! My wonderment took no more than half a minute. It sure was bitter blowing.

I'd have to face the weather getting home, though. No way to avoid it—the only path into the arms of my lounge chair was walking back out through that air. So I braced myself.

Nothing prepared me for stepping outside again. That wind! It was steep, high, mountainous, by the feel of it. A solid wall of wind. I could see Jim Titus going by, bowing as he walked on into it, his jacket bellied out behind him.

"Having weather today!" he shouted.

Starting up the car took me some minutes. The motor

was cold. I kept grinding until it took hold, and, even then, I waited, running it in place to make sure it wouldn't quit on me. Even with the windshield wipers going I couldn't see much, so I swiped at the inside fog with my hands—a little better—then shifted to second and eased out onto the road.

The road was near empty, and no wonder, the wind— chill as an arctic blast—mean and meaner as I went along. I'd rolled up my window tight, but it still got to me, shaking the car from side to side and, once, making me swag sharp to the left. Like somebody—actual hands—took ahold of the steering wheel. Everything was bent and twisted with that wind, the prairie grass, the few trees, the mesquite—but mesquite always looks like that, snarled and trying to slither free, like it's in a mess of pain. The sight of it brought my morning mood back to me. Sometimes, when I was feeling old, achy and cranky as I did then, I thought a fast emergency would be better than this long dull time. I was ready to go.

Soon as that thought crossed my mind, I regretted it. Because what I saw next numbed me to the bone. Like that very idea took flesh from my thinking on it. Had to draw up sharp, side of the road, turn on my hazards and slow my blinking breath. That plane I'd wondered at only minutes before, it was coming down—slamming down— in yonder field. Must of spun—one wing touched first. Must of tumbled—a great big bucketing noise. Then I couldn't see to tell. Something burst—spewed out—fire and smoke rushed to swallow the ground. It all happened so quick. So quick, I heard myself trying to talk it back up —"Wait wait wait—"

Didn't call on the Lord, or anyone. Nobody to call on. Couldn't think. People, live people inside. Freeze and look on. Smoke so clotted I didn't know how anybody could make it out alive.

It was *my* field where the plane had come down. We'd named it "Hannah's field," for Troy's mother. Half a section north by northwest, furrowed, pre-watered, ready for seeding. Meant for milo, any day Bud Pearson saw fit now. That was the only thought I could go on with. Couldn't get over it being my own field—the rest was too much for me, so I fixed on that. The plane had barely missed my stubble field, and my set-aside, which I'd planted to love grass, all dry now. Crashing down in either of those would of burnt up everything twice, plane, house, shed. It was like I'd laid out that field and delayed planting it for knowing something like this would come along. Like the field had been just waiting.

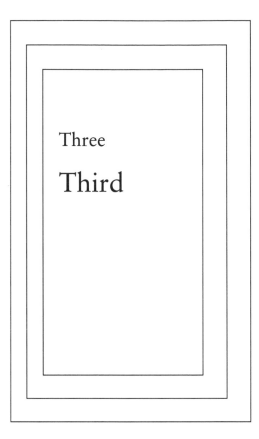

Three

Third

MY DAY OFF, as it happened. I was heading north. Hunting for some easy listening on the radio, I remember saying to myself, *must be getting old—can't tell the music from the static anymore.* But maybe it was the weather. Crazy to be out in it if you didn't have to be. Normally, I wouldn't, but I'd sniffed out a bargain. It was too good a deal to wait.

So I was on my way, hoping to get a jump on the competition. My destination, I thought, was Hardesty, and my aim was to follow up on this ad for a power drill set, slightly used but in mint condition. The owner and I had gone over most of the details on the phone. I'm an amateur carpenter. I like building things—birdhouses, doghouses, swing sets, toolsheds, you name it. It's a hobby, one of my few pastimes, and I don't mind selling a thing or two on the side. Selling isn't the point, though.

I guess, too, it was the idea of getting out, getting away. Nothing to beat home for. I was at the end of one thing and not so sure it was the beginning of anything else. I'd done my share of playing around, but this was the first time since my divorce that I'd been seriously involved with a woman, the third time in my life—counting marriage—that I'd ever laid myself open to real hurt. Then the whole living-together, playing-married thing had suddenly, silently, fizzled out, as if nothing had ever been. She'd finished packing by the time I came in from work, and was in a tearing rush to be gone. Said something on the stairs I didn't catch, something about explaining later, getting in touch soon. I thought I was entitled to know more: "What does that mean—*soon?*" I stood on the landing and yelled down the stairwell. Needn't of bothered. She mumbled something under her breath, sounded like "tomorrow, this weekend, whenever." She'd left behind the milk-frothing pan from her cappuccino machine and her curling iron. That was two weeks ago. Not a word since. I'd be damned if I'd call *her*. I had a certain pride, after all, and I've never liked games. So much for the "free and easy" life— where's the easy in it?

I'm from Philadelphia originally. "Damnyankee," as

they say in Texas. (That's one and the same word.) Most
people here can spot the strangeness right off the bat, even
after all these years. What brought me out to this part of
the country was not so original: it was job opportunity,
I'd researched it. Fort Worth is city, not great big or great
anything, but trying to think well of itself. Far less hassle
than any city of comparable size I knew of in the East. So I
stayed, stayed on—what?—going on fourteen years now.
A stretch . . .

I always get spooked out by long country drives anywhere north or west of Fort Worth. So vast a nothing—
mile upon mile upon mile with only the wind for company. The wind, and maybe a bunch of box-headed cattle
clumped nose to nose along the fence wire, taking note of
my passing, eager for events. I like long views, like being
able to "see out," as they say, but in moderation, not
being able to see out *forever*. No place to hide is the feeling. Unsheltered—no hills or coves to hood yourself with,
no place to take cover. Wherever you'd run, it'd be the
same: empty land sinking under its load of sky. Even on a
sunny day—and most of our days are sunny here—I get
spooked.

Anyway . . . it sure wasn't sunny out then. It was ut-
terly cheerless, dark, dank. "Falling weather" the locals
call it—something, no telling what, waiting to fall on us.
Visibility was minimal. Couldn't put a measure to it, it
varied, but there wasn't much of any kind of view. Every
time the wind struck up, it crossed my mind how crazy it
was to be venturing out on a day like this. But I'd commit-
ted myself, I was nearly there—

At that moment, I was getting set to pass an ancient

driver, who was blundering along in a vintage pickup. Looked like something out of *The Grapes of Wrath,* except it was empty. Why they permit antiques like that to circulate on public highways is a mystery to me. He was lazing along at tractor speed.

I only remember something so trifling now because of what came afterwards. I sped up a little, fuming to get free of him. Checking the rearview mirror before returning to my lane, I saw something that drew me up sharp onto the median. Good thing it was grassy!

What I saw in the mirror was a plume of black smoke. By the time I'd turned my head to get a better look, it had thickened to a funnel. Four stories high, I'd say, and rising. Coming from someplace a little north, northwest of town.

Slow as it was, that pickup must have passed me while I was gawking; there wasn't a trace of him when I started up again. I drove on ahead about a quarter mile, took a U-turn at the first crossover, then headed back the way I'd come. I kept that cloud, still rising, in my sights.

Kept wondering which of the few poor industries in Bounds could put up a blaze like that. Damned if I knew. I could tick off the local industries on the fingers of one hand, actually. There was livestock trucking, a pet food factory, couple of seed and feed companies, what else? Windmill blades—I should have thought of that first. I'd once written a feature on that, on the importance of windmills to ranching on the high plains . . . And there was salvage—combine, tractor, hot rod—plenty of salvage sold in Bounds. That shouldn't really count as industry, though; they didn't convert salvage into anything else—all they did was sell it.

Anything more?

Along with ditching and irrigation pit cleaning, I couldn't think of a thing. None of those industries, short of a bomb, could have caused an explosion like this. The cloud was taller than the grain elevator by then, and that elevator was the only high-rise in Bounds, a good—what —five, six stories?

I'd been in Bounds before, spent nearly half a year in the area as a regional reporter in my cub days. I was a kid on my first beat, still milky behind the ears, and everything was new. I worked hard. Got to know every cat and dog in town on a first-name basis, yet never had any idea what the people in Bounds thought about to themselves all day long. No idea! *Did* they think? You had to wonder. Did they still list each and every pallbearer in their obituary notices like they used to? Most likely—what other news had they besides funerals and weather? There surely wasn't a whole lot doing in Bounds back then, except for the Oktoberfest, the Baptist fish fry, 4-H showmanship at the County Fair, or the Girl Scouts having a manicure party and who sold the most Golden Yangles. Dan Lutes, one of the local boys, played for the Dallas Cowboys—a tackle back in the early '80s. He was the town's only claim to fame. And—speaking of the devil—

There it was, still standing. Same old sign in front of the town hall, a bit faded but the same: BOUNDS, TEXAS—HOME OF DAN LUTES OF THE DALLAS COWBOYS. What a crock! Dan left town after high school, hadn't been back since, and the rest of his family moved out a couple years after he did.

The power lines were cut on Bowie, one dangling low, a live-wire hazard. The stoplight whipped on its cable, the poles that held it tethered rocking and groaning in the wind, everything unstable. The big old elms looked shredded: a litter of small branches scattered over the road like the palsied spill from a matchbox or a wild throw of fortune-telling sticks. No way to avoid them and spare the tires.

Corner of First and Longview, all the traffic lights were down. What to do? Look three ways and go, only thing to do. I passed the site of the old Gilbreath place. There'd been some changes, I noticed. The building was now a senior citizens center. Gilbreath's was the general store in my day. Used to advertise: *From the cradle to the grave, we meet all your needs.* Can't get much more general than that. They sold everything. Then got sold, apparently. Must be a lot of senior citizens here now, I reflected, and not a great many cradles. The young move on.

I was on my way out of town. Got the feeling I'd passed a wrong way sign back there somewhere—quite a number of wrong way signs. Nobody around, nobody stirring, everything with its back turned to me. Heading north on a southbound lane was the feeling, like a bad dream. All alone and ass-backwards.

No hope of asking directions either. I didn't want to lose a minute, so I kept on moving, heading due north. When I passed the church with a peeling roof and a short ladder of bells for a steeple, I had my bearings. This would be Blessed Redeemer on Eighth and Longview. You can always recognize an R.C. establishment by the statues, this one no exception. Some stone saint posted out in front, his raised hand rigid in benediction. *No, no—thanks, but no*—I scooted on by.

Bounds used to have about twelve hundred households, going by the gas meter count. When I asked people what the population was, they'd usually say: "Depends on whether you're coming or going." And they'd laugh, though it wasn't a joke. For a fact, the numbers on the signs standing at the north and south city limits didn't match. I'd have to ferret the figures out.

I kept moving in the direction of that cloud. It was looser and broader at the top now, starting to lean a little in the direction of the prevailing wind. The road ahead continued to be deserted. I jumped a stop sign—daring, wishing, somebody would challenge me. I'd of welcomed the police, but they, along with everybody else, seemed to be inside—"weathered in," as they'd say—or busy elsewhere.

Already, I was making mental notes. Even then, I could see the story in my mind's eye: cut line, lead line, inches allotted. I'd have to phone it in, assuming the phones were working. Call Mo to summon the troops. But first I'd have to get there myself, see what was what.

Soon as I turned into the old Farm-to-Market Road, I didn't have to keep my eyes on anything but the faded yellow line in front of me. If I'd been walking, I could have made it there blindfolded. My eyes stung and blurred as I pressed on into the thick of it. Couldn't miss it. All I had to do was to follow my nose.

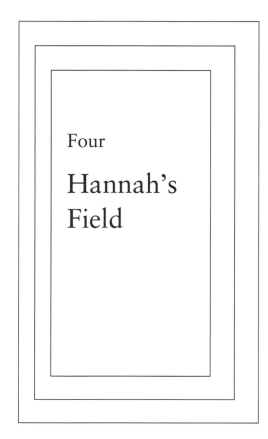

Four

Hannah's Field

NO PLACE you can go nowadays, howsoever far, without the world raining in on you! And I don't mean the television only, or hometown boys called up to service half the world away, but right here. Take a little small place nobody ever heard of, like Bounds. Right here in Bounds in my own backyard—the whole world raining in!

I'm none too proud of it, but that was my next long thought—furious—watching the smoke pour out of my field, watching the clouds thick up, the smoke blacken. Maybe it was a respite from asking myself what on earth I could do for them and knowing it was nothing, not one blessed thing for now.

Then I picked up car sounds, slow and grinding, in the distance. Coming my way. I thought I knew whose pickup that would be, could of had RESCUE blazoned all over it, my heart warmed so. Sure enough, it was Jim Titus. He drew up behind me and got out. I cranked down my window. He stood alongside, gazing ahead as I was.

Finally he said, "Why don't you go on ahead. Be careful, keep your eye on the wind. You should be all right. I'll meet you over there in a little bit." He started away, then halted and called over his shoulder, "Might be a good idea to gather up all the blankets in the house."

"I'll do that."

"Oh, and Glenna"—he turned again—"you might fetch a hatchet while you're at it."

Hatchet? I wondered about that, but nodded. Had to use my left hand to unpeel the fingers of my right off of the steering wheel and onto the ignition, that's how clenched they were. How numb. Shifting gear, I missed, hit the windshield wipers instead. Sat back stunned for a moment—unable to break the chattering spell of it, and nothing else but that sweeping and canceling, that dry scraping, in my mind.

Coming up to the house, all I could see was this huge, rolling fire in the middle of the field, smoke streaming, and, closer to the edge, little pointed blades of flame. The house was safe for the time being, but here, too, the electricity was down—phone dead, lights out. I busied myself searching for flashlights and a kerosene lamp, and set them out on the foyer table where I'd be able to find them in the dark. Then I gathered up my spare blankets and stashed them under the table. I fetched the hatchet from the basement, trying not to picture what it was for. When I ventured out of doors again, I didn't get far. There was still too much smoke to be able to see much, wind-driven smoke and the wind wild, no telling which direction from minute to minute. I started coughing, my eyes filled and wouldn't stop. Best wait for Jim inside, I told myself. But, back in the house, I couldn't sit. I stood behind the door where I had a small lookout window. I paced.

I was thinking on my number four well, three hundred and fifty gallons per minute, how, if I could reach Bud Pearson, we could make a set and flood the field. Would that help, or just make a mess, the mud running like slush underfoot? Maybe the fire department would rather use the well as backup. I needed to ask somebody, but there was no sign of Jim Titus yet, nor the help he'd gone after. Couldn't of taken but minutes, yet felt like forever.

Then I spotted Jim's pickup with the county sheriff's car in tow, and the Bounds fire department, our one yellow truck, not far behind. Not long after that, the ambulance from Hardesty County Hospital raced up, with lights, sirens, everything blaring. They all parked snub up to the fence line, real close to one another, so I knew they were making room for more to come. They didn't glance in the direction of the house, but I decided to brew some coffee for when they did. When it looked like they wouldn't be coming inside anytime in the next few hours, I filled a big thermos with coffee, took up my bundle of blankets, and went out to them.

The smoke was still pretty fierce. I kept my head down. Ahead was a dark oily billowing that set my eyes to stinging. Our little fire wagon from Bounds was working, best it could, on the biggest and loudest blaze—part of the passenger cabin. They churned up a lot of spray. Wherever the water gushed, steam spouted up, then flame again. You couldn't hear anything but roaring—wind, water, blaze.

I stood with the ambulance crew from Hardesty. They were waiting for the fire department to give them a sign to go forward. "Will you lookit there!" one of the nurses pointed, "See them? And that there—take a look at him!" When the wind caved a clearing in the smoke, I tried to make out what she was seeing—people who'd crawled out of chinks in the cabin wall, or jumped somehow. Or been thrown like rag dolls, and now lay sprawled out all over the field. A few were upright, stumbling around, and one man was actually walking. Imagine: walking! He was moving fast. We hailed him—one of the crew jumped the fence and ran after him. "What in hell do you think you're doing?" someone standing close to me hollered, "You've gotta wait—" But the man he was hailing seemed not to hear; he stopped halfway to the cabin and made a sign to the rest of the crew: three fingers, held high. Three or four, who could tell? It was a count, I suppose, a body count. He waved the others to come forward. Nobody budged. "Wait till it cooks off!" a nurse yelled to him. *Cooks off!* —what a thing to say. There was a sudden waterfall of flame, then smoke gushed from the cabin and gusted over the field—covering people, rubble, earth—you couldn't see a thing. It was hard to breathe. We all turned to face the house till it cleared.

I wish I'd turned for good and gone back into the house. Instead, I lingered on. There was the passenger cabin, what was left of it, slowly caving in on itself. The Bounds fire truck was backing up to get clear of it. Beyond the sounds of water pounding, metal twisting and grinding, the hissing of steam, I thought I could make out cries, faint cries.

Then I wasn't sure. There seemed nothing human left in the field. Only mineral, metal, cuttings, shreddings of things—and the wind.

Must of been bitter cold standing there at the fence, but somehow I'd clean forgotten to notice. Or maybe the heat from the fire was drifting to us. More ambulances came wailing in, from Story and Fescue, and another town, a name I didn't catch. A helicopter alighted in a far corner of the field, yet more noise—it hardly mattered—added to the din.

The first out-of-town newspaper reporter was already on the scene, shifting from one person to the next. Before long, he was onto me. He started asking me what I'd seen and when, and jotting it down. I can't imagine I said as much as he seemed to be writing. Passing time, I guess, till the smoke cleared and he could angle in for a closer look. I offered him coffee and he seemed glad of it. Jim Titus joined us. I mentioned flooding the field, using my number four well, but Jim advised me to wait until I was asked.

We were still just mainly waiting. The reporter inquired of Jim whether there wasn't a minister to be had in town. Only two full-time, Jim explained, the rest coming and going. Jim took the hint, though, and went off to fetch whichever one of them happened to be on hand. Another ambulance blazed in, another fire truck—bigger than anything I'd ever seen in the county. The firemen had taken down most of the fence by then, so they drove right up onto the field. They straddled along the furrows, getting in as close as they could.

The smoke had thinned out. I could see the cockpit with its roof blown away, sucked full of earth, a jagged ditch sawed deeply in the ground—I tried not to think of it as my field or Hannah's field. Or my shed—the tailpiece standing slap up against the wall of it. Not far from the tailpiece was a wing, what was left. Wasn't a trace of the other wing from where I stood.

The passenger cabin came to three chunks. The biggest of them had melted down into itself. Nothing left now but the bare blackened frame of it. I'd seen that happen with my own eyes. Those openings were windows once.

Somebody—looked like an officer from the State Highway Patrol—ordered me to stand back. "This area is off bounds to visitors," is what he said. "How about it being *my* land and off bounds to trespassers!" I let him have it then. "Can't stop you if that's the case," he said, "but you'll wish I had." I stood my ground at the fence line. I didn't step forward, though.

Now that the smoke had cleared, the ambulance people were out there in force. They'd put down blankets, my four among them, and were laying people longwise, one on each. And—I wasn't imagining this—quite a number of passengers were walking. Couldn't mistake who they were: they were staggering, lurching off in all directions, their clothes in shreds, their faces streaked with blood or oil. "In shock," a nurse explained to me. "They must be made to lie down. Lie down or pay later. They *must.*"

One of the ambulances started unloading backboards and neck braces—must of been a hundred of those things. Then came the television crews with all their lights and gear, then more police cars from out of town, flashers whirling. The tiredness got to me finally, end of my second wind. I was just taking a peek at the shed before starting back up towards the house when I heard somebody dogging my steps. I jolted around, surprised—

The others too busy to notice, I guess.

He was an old man in a good suit and a neat blue tie, the stub of it, sheared off maybe an inch under the knot. He was padding along in his sock feet. Nothing about him seemed touched or shaken, nothing but a thumbprint of kerosene, a little mark like a badge, on his cheek. "Bitteh," he said. Or "Bitter"—I wasn't sure. He said it again, but more like a question, "Bitter?" He was breathing hard, his face flushed with effort, and his eyes were roaming, wild.

"Should you be walking around just yet?" I asked. He had this dipping walk, or maybe it was from making his way across the furrows. He didn't take any notice of my question, so I gave him the answer myself: "I don't think so—I don't think it's wise."

He stopped and stared at me then, like I was somebody he knew well whose name he had mislaid. "Don't worry," he said to me. He had an accent—German, foreign, something; the way he said "worry," I could tell. "Baggage is no problem now," he said.

Five

Eyewitness News

THIS IS WHAT the eyewitnesses said they saw:

—"It was going along real quiet. Low, I thought, but quiet, then the engines got real loud. Then quiet again, like they'd shut off. Damn thing slammed into the ground, then exploded."

—"It just hung there and exploded in the air."

—"The plane was burning when it came down, streaming black smoke. It nose-dived right fucking smack into the ground. Couldn't believe my eyes!"

—"I'd say it pancaked. Sinking, more than diving. You know? Didn't see any fire till it hit."

—"It was banking right when it plunged. On fire? I could swear to it!"

—"I was standing at Allsup's looking south when I saw it. It was flying level as I recollect, then all of a sudden it disappeared. It was just 'crump!'—this little small sound. And that was it. It was gone."

I could swear to this—I could swear to that—*"with my own eyes, I saw it!"* That's how it always is with one event seen through different windows. My job is sifting it. I figured the stall was probably right; there'd been time enough for a lot of people to see whatever it was they saw. I hadn't a clue as to whether the plane was in flames before it fell: I'd only become aware of things after the aircraft was down, a huge arrow of smoke pointing to the spot. Anyway, most people get the impact-fire sequence backwards, I've learned since. They tend to see fire first because it's what they expect to see.

I borrowed a cellular phone from a county official and got through to Mo Burns, my bureau chief. "Where *are* you?" he asked. "Bounds—Bounds, Texas," I repeated; the reception was hit and miss. "Refresh my memory— where is that?" he asked. So I did my best to place it on the map. "Okay, got it—got it, so you're out in the boonies, but you've got a big-time story, could be one helluva story, and you're the first reporter on the scene. It's our scoop! So talk—talk it in—tell me what you see. Let me just— Okay, I'm ready. Shoot—"

I wasn't able to see anything much right yet, I explained. There was still too much smoke.

"Send a photographer," I urged him, "send two." But Mo was already onto that, I felt sure, his adrenaline surging, figuring how to keep an edge on the media people with their sound cameras and live, up-to-the-minute, transmission capacities. They were sure to arrive soon, and, soon as they did, we'd be playing second fiddle. Yet, for the moment, it was, like Mo said, our scoop. I fancied I could hear Mo ticking off a mental list of assignments: Sue to the Dallas-Fort Worth airport. Bill to the county morgue in Hardesty. Cubs to the area hospitals with burn units. Somebody would be writing a backgrounder, one of the interns, most likely. *Major Crashes in North Texas*— something along those lines. We have quite a file in the library, waiting around for occasions like this.

Mo wanted figures—injuries, fatalities, survivors. Walk-aways, if any. And he wanted impressions: fire, smoke, debris, human interest angles, the *feel* of the scene. The space for that would only come after the factual news-briefs were in place, but he wanted me to start jotting things down now.

Mo didn't have to tell me what to notice. I'd never covered an air crash before, but I'd done countless auto collisions and a bus crash. And plenty of fires. Anyway, I'd been a reporter long enough—I'd "been around." My mind works the same way as his.

Still, Mo kept harping on the numbers. The way he

carried on, he made a mystique of it. "There are exact numbers," he insisted. "The airline officials are going to fudge them, do everything they can to hide them. You've got to hound those people, keep after them."

Actually, the number Mo most wanted didn't exist yet. Not the fatality count—or, if it did—only in the mind of God. Meanwhile, there'd be all kinds of other numbers to ferret out. I jotted down a quick list. First off—and even that wouldn't be easy—was a count of passengers on board. Sue, or whoever was assigned to the airport, would be better placed to press the airline officials for that figure. There'd be the number of survivors, injured, feared dead, confirmed dead. Then the missing and unaccounted for—

But there were no numbers to be had that afternoon. If any officials of the airline were on site, they didn't declare themselves. I did as well as I could with the little I had for the first two stories. Since I couldn't make out what I was seeing with any clarity, I stuck to the barest facts.

I filed the first story at 3:45 p.m.:

> BOUNDS, TEXAS—A jet described as a 727 plowed into a field outside of Bounds, Texas and burst into flames shortly after 2 p.m. this afternoon.
>
> Glenna B. Wooten, an eyewitness, said she had noticed the plane "flying too low for a big jet" shortly before the crash.
>
> There was no immediate word on casualties.

By five, Sue's report from DFW had come in. We still didn't have even a tentative survivor and casualty count and, of course, no names yet, but the carrier company had acknowledged the crash and claimed to be at work trying to ascertain the numbers. Since the figures Mo wanted weren't forthcoming, the paper ended up doing a recap of an earlier crash of a plane from the same carrier company, same make aircraft, and trotted out the numbers on that. He's a nut on numbers, Mo is.

Our combined report, Sue's and mine, looked like information. It came to six inches, double column, with a sidebar on 727 crashes, and graphics. They ran it front page on the late evening edition. It *looked* like information, but we still didn't know a damn thing.

BOUNDS, TEXAS—A Maxim 727 jet crashed thirty minutes after takeoff from the Dallas-Fort Worth International Airport this afternoon. Maxim officials said the plane was Flight 582 en route to Kennedy Airport in New York. It carried 92 passengers and 7 crew members. The flight originated in San Diego.

"There appear to be a number of survivors," said Maxim official Jeff Loring. He was unable to give a casualty count at this time.

Several eyewitnesses said that they had seen the plane in apparent trouble shortly before the crash. "It was flying way too low and seemed to be in a stall," said Jim Titus, an electrician in Bounds.

The plane plowed into the dirt of a pasture and exploded in flames.

"I was heading home from work when I saw the plane coming down," said Glenna B. Wooten, postmaster of Bounds. "It was too slow before—then too fast. It came down flat in the middle of my field."

"You hear about this on the news, but you never think it will come home to you," Mrs. Wooten said. She farms a section and a half of land on the outskirts of Bounds. The field where the 727 crashed is furrowed and ready for planting milo. "We were a little late this year, on account of the frost," Mrs. Wooten explained.

The accident is the second for Maxim since its founding last year.

On September 17, 1990, Maxim Flight 323 crashed on takeoff from Tampa Bay, Florida, killing 113 people, including 4 crew members.

Investigators of that crash determined that birds sucked into the right engine disabled the plane, depriving it of lifting power.

Six

Triage

TURNING UP THE ROAD to Blessed Redeemer, I wasn't thinking about the plane. All I had in mind during the last lap of the drive was getting home, and how happy I would be indoors, out of the weather. I was—plenty happy. Grateful to have arrived without incident. I stooped for my mail in the foyer. More of the usual: a heap of catalogs, religious supply, publishers. A bill for utilities I wasn't eager to face, but nothing could touch my mood. Or so I thought . . .

The electricity seemed to be out. No problem: I fetched the kerosene lamp from the kitchen and lit it. It was warm enough in the living room—I'd left my gas heater on since the night before. I was about to settle down in comfort, when I heard someone pounding on the door.

It was Jim Titus. He's not Catholic, but everybody knows Jim. "Better come along with me, Father," he said without preamble, "no time to explain now." So I reached for my coat again; I'd only had time enough to toss it over a chair.

"Better bring all your gear—whatever it is. It's a pretty big accident," Jim added. "Other pastor's out of town. You're the only one on hand."

"Take me a couple of minutes," I told him. "Why don't you come on inside and warm up?" But he only motioned over his shoulder to his pickup. Said he'd be waiting for me in it—he'd left his motor running.

I made my way back to the sacristy for the oil. Jim hadn't taken the trouble to spell out what the appropriate "gear" might be. It wasn't necessary: I knew he meant last rites.

The fire was down to smolderings when we arrived. It would gust up in scattered points here and there, then subside. Smoke poured from the field—yellow, gray, black and oily brown—from plastics, metal, fuel burning. The smog of their blending set us to clearing our throats and rubbing our eyes. The fences were down, I noticed. We followed the bright orange edge-markers laid down by the police, driving right onto the field, across the furrows—a rugged ride.

We were stopped a ways off from the main wreckage by a man in uniform. State Highway Patrol—I guess they were using everybody they could find. I explained why I'd come and how I'd be wanting to get in close as I could. "Plenty of work for you right here, Father." The officer opened both arms wide. "Okay," I agreed, "I'll start here." I could make out seat stuffing, wires, shredded metal, paper money blowing, mud darkened with oil. A clutch of fur—looked like a cat caught in a combine; a plastic comb. I stepped gingerly, watchfully; there were, as I feared, human fragments, clumps of human meat, underfoot. An arm or armrest so charred I couldn't tell which. What to do? You don't anoint or absolve fragments. You don't let them simply lie around for the bulldozer, either. So I stood there in the mud, making the sign of the cross and speaking into that smoke-fouled air the words of general conditional absolution. "If you are disposed, I absolve you . . ." Then riffled through the pages of the ritual for a blessing specific to the scene before me, struck for the first time by how white, how unstained, those pages were. Where was the blessing, prayer—any prayer at all that might remotely apply to this? *Guide and provision them . . . Protect . . . restore . . . relieve . . .* Nothing—it was all bruise balm, mild, bland, skin-deep— *Shelter . . . enfold . . . enclose . . .* nothing doing.

But I stared at the one that followed. It would have to do:

Lord, hear our prayers and be merciful
to your son (daughter) N., whom you have called from
this life

Welcome him (her) into the company of your saints,
in the kingdom of light and peace.
(We ask this) through Christ our Lord—

I saw bright hair—a woman's head, tumbled like a melon, in a ditch—*even the hairs of your head are counted* —a man's shoe, a new loafer, elegantly tasseled, the foot still in it.

I said what I could:

"Father, these were human beings. You made them. You loved them. You alone know who they are. Gather them up. Be merciful. Welcome them . . ." On the words "light and peace" I faltered, though.

Then I headed for the triage area, where paramedics were busy laying out passengers on colored blankets. The rule of triage is to abandon the dead and set the dying aside, the better to tend to those with a fighting chance of recovery. It didn't sound merciful, but I knew it was, a way of distributing mercy, medical mercy, as efficiently as possible.

I was the inefficient one, tending to the dying first. They were unaware; most of them would never know that I'd been there beside them. I had no idea how many of them were Catholics, and God alone knew how many of the Catholics among them were fit to receive absolution and the sacrament.

God knew—I didn't. I didn't presume to know. I anointed anyone who stirred, trembled, breathed or seemed to breathe. Anyone and everyone. Err on the side of lavishness, I'd been taught. Anoint conditionally. Leave it to the Lord to sort it out.

One of the nurses called over to me to get gloves on; they were all wearing them. I pretended I hadn't heard. I'd read about a priest once who'd administered last rites with tongs. It had been a bad case, to be sure, but I couldn't ever see doing that. Anointing, it seemed to me, had to be done with living hands, with hands of flesh.

Nothing I'd ever encountered before had prepared me for what I was to meet here. I'd seen death often enough, but this was a battlefield.

"If you are alive, I pray—" This was the formula. He was a young man, living or dead, I could not tell. His face and arm muscles still moved, but he wasn't breathing that I could see. If in doubt, anoint. I did. "Through this holy anointing may the Lord in His love and mercy help you." When I touched his forehead, his mouth opened. I glanced away—not soon enough. How black it was, gobbed with mud, or blood— "With the grace of the Holy Spirit . . ." I needed that grace, too.

There was a child, a pretty thing with dark curls. Unspotted—not a mark on her. She was warm yet, but motionless, absolutely still. No one's found out so far, was my first thought. But, no, more likely, someone had and, unable to concede death, left her among the lingering. I anointed her as well.

A woman after that. A ring on her finger caught the light, shone with a fractured brilliance. But her face was clouded, drawn, her eyes shut. She was making no sound. I tried to tell her that she had permission to speak, to weep, to scream, anything she had the strength for. No response; I assumed there was no strength to spare. When I touched her hands, though, she shook mine off with a force that surprised me. I persisted, anointing the backs of her hands, her forehead, speaking the words of absolution: "May the Lord who frees you from sin save you and raise you up." Before leaving, I touched her shoulder lightly, the way friends do. She opened her eyes at that—I don't know what she was seeing then. "That you, dear?" she asked. "Joe? That you?" Then her eyes froze. I put my face close to hers to check for breathing, but she was gone.

My hands unsteady, I had to pause before going on.

After I'd worked over the triage area, I wandered around some more in the muck. There were medics everywhere, moving slowly, four to a litter, stooping for vital signs, saying the same words over and over: "Easy there. Lie still. I'm coming. Breathe nice and easy now, nice and easy"—a litany of sorts. I headed for the far edge of the field, searching for anyone they might have missed. I spotted what I was looking for pretty quickly.

He was sitting there, off a little to one side, squatting on the ground, his back up against the tail of the plane. Strangely, no fire had touched that part of the tail, its long flank clean and cool, its crosspiece, shaping the letter "T," standing perfectly plum. Out of range of the emergency lights, and all the motion and commotion in the center of the field, the scene here was dim, almost peaceful.

I could make him out as clearly as if there'd been a spotlight on him, a halo of distress maybe, a spiky radiance. As close to inanimate as a breathing thing could be —flesh masquerading as chunk of metal or stone. *Posttraumatic stress syndrome,* I think they call it. As if that could explain a thing.

Coming closer, I noticed he was moving ever so slightly,

nursing his cheek with one hand. I waved to him as I approached.

Nothing. He didn't blink, even. I was only a few yards off by then, and there was still no sign that he was aware of me, not the faintest tremor. His eyes stared straight ahead, fixed on my approach, but seemed veiled. I advanced slowly. At least he hadn't warned me off—I'd given him ample time for it.

A man in his sixties or seventies. Didn't look to be a scratch on him. He was listening intently to something, one hand cradling his cheek. Mouth-speaking-to-ear is what it looked like. His other hand remained inert, loosely capping one knee.

"Hello there!" I called over, maybe too brightly. "You all right?"

He was trying to cover his mouth with his cheek hand. It occurred to me that he might have broken his jaw or lost some teeth. "You all right?" I raised my voice. "Anybody tended to you yet?" I stooped forward, maybe two feet from his face. He couldn't mistake who it was I was talking to.

He coughed—a long thick monosyllable. I noticed the forced lift of his collarbone, and imagined he was straining to clear his throat.

"Cough drop?" I offered. I fished in my pocket for the box I usually carry in winter. "Here, take this—" I tapped out a lozenge.

To my amazement, he moved, released the hand from his knee, and stretched it out to me. Took and ate. A great loosening followed: he flexed one foot, then the other, he unclasped his hand from his cheek. Made a fist, then opened it, curling and uncurling his fingers. He performed these motions with painstaking slowness and attentiveness, as though working out the logistics for the first time. Then he coughed again, releasing his voice. It was whispery, gruff, at first. Hard to make out what he was saying. "See, no," was what it sounded like.

"Please?" I said. "I didn't catch—"

He cleared his throat, shaking his head this time, and blurting out, "I didn't die then?"

I assured him that he was most certainly alive.

"Well, I'll be damned," he said.

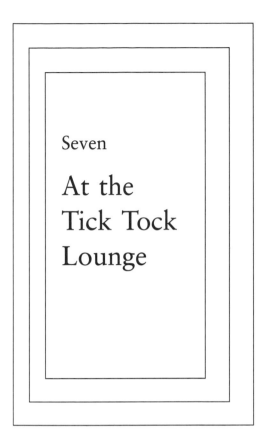

Seven

At the Tick Tock Lounge

FIND YOUR OWN FUN or do without is how I get along in Bounds. I make my time pass, as best as possible. Sometimes I like to take a break from my dogs and get off to a place where I can study human nature. Not mix with it—study it. I don't get thick with anyone. When trouble pops open, I'm not there.

Any honky-tonk would do, but Tick Tock Lounge is closest, not but six miles over the county line. Bounds is in

Manifest—a dry county, so you gotta get cross that line. Whitney Olsen opened up Tick Tock to fill the need. He knows me, Whitney does, he's bought a number of dogs off of me over the years. I raise Blue Heeler pups for herding, German Shepherds and such—working dogs, mostly, but also a few recreational types. I gave Whitney one of those for a pet he keeps back out at the house. That's Salsa, a Mexican Hairless *with* hair, the one out of four in the litter that's got more than fuzz. I prefer them without hair, myself. Why? Just do.

Anyhoo—Buck, one of my stud dogs, had died on me about an hour before. I'd taken him to the vet with what I thought was worms, and ended up having to put him to sleep in my lap. I wasn't in the finest of moods and I thought a couple of beers would help.

Whitney reads me pretty good. He says, "Hi, Chip," and I say, "Hey," and he says, "What d'ya know?" and I say, "Not a whole bunch." And that's it—I'm off the hook.

Then I find myself a booth and order a pitcher of fresh draw. I settle in. Sit there, real quiet, slowly getting buzzed, till I've had enough (beer and eavesdropping) and I'm ready to go back to my dogs again. That's what I was intending to do the afternoon Buck died. Afternoon of the crash, but I didn't know that yet. It was right after the electricity came back on.

Old Jack Henderson was sitting on one of the high stools, his nose buried in a newspaper already out of date. Jack wasn't drinking anything and hadn't so much as blinked when I came in. Whitney was hassling him about it, trying to snag his attention. "Anything new?" he asked.

Jack shook his head. "Anything good?" Jack shook his head again. Jack's a welder, use to be, but he's been retired for some time now. He lives down the street from the lounge. Comes in for company since his old lady passed on. You'd never know it from the sound of him that he's here to be social. But look who's talking—he's about as gassy as I am.

The electricity had come back on around four, a little after four. The television screens up above the bar were still blank when I came in, though. I found my booth and settled. Whitney was busy tending. Then he went up to the sets, lifting his remote to one and the other, igniting the screens. Somebody clapped.

It was Channel Four news. "High wind events" were top of the list. Downed power lines, power outages. "We've had wind blowing down lines, wind blowing debris onto lines, wind knocking trees into lines"—it was somebody from the utility company speaking. "Keep the kiddies indoors," he warned. "If you see anything dangling, assume it's live. Thing to do is stay away from it. Don't touch it, and don't touch anything it's touching."

More on the wind—they were reporting gusts of up to sixty miles an hour north of Hardesty. Man on the news was saying he'd heard of a stop sign chasing a dumpster down the main street in Tattle, Texas. Must of been a sight —a stop sign that wouldn't stop. Or tall tale, I bet. There weren't any pictures.

The news all seemed to be about weather—weather related. A pile-up on the Interstate. A closeup of that. Some loose steers—"cattle on the lam," the announcer called it, trying to be cute. They gave us a shot of that—of rear ends

bumping along Farm-to-Market Road. Nothing too un-
usual there. When the wind blows really hard and the
electrified fences go dead, cattle walk over the wire and
take off for themselves. Happens in blizzards quite a bit.

Paul Plemons, the brand inspector, was reported to be
tracking the steers back to their owners, but the county
sheriff, who should of been in on it, was somewheres else
on call. I didn't wonder about the missing sheriff much as
I might of at that moment.

It was early yet. The lounge was pretty well near empty.
Besides Jack Henderson, there were a couple of regulars
from the feedyard, drinking beer at the other end of the
bar, and somebody I didn't recognize, some hippie-dip
type with long hair, shooting pool by himself in the back.
There were two total strangers in the booth ahead of
mine, a man and a woman. City people, from the looks of
them, people passing through. Must of come in out of the
weather. Separate cars probably. They were more than
strangers to each other, less than friends. Might of met up
right here on the parking lot. Come in out of the wind and
killing time, I guessed. They weren't traveling together
and wouldn't grieve if their paths never crossed again—
that was my reading of it. They were sipping coffee from
beer mugs.

I just let my ears hang down and listen.

"St. Louis is where I'm from but, you name it—New
York, Chicago, Detroit—I've been there," the man said.
"I've been to Europe, too. Rome. Paris. London. The Near
East. The Far East. Even been to Tibet, but you can have
it. Everything there smells of yak butter."

Seemed like they'd been talking for a good long while.

Or the man had—sort of petting his own hair with talk. He was on a roll, the woman listening, or pretending to, nodding and putting in a word edgewise now and then to show she was awake. I missed the thread of what he was trying to say. That happens often but, if I stay tuned, I usually catch on sooner or later. Tick Tock is the perfect place for listening in; they don't have a jukebox to drown everything out, and the high backs of the booths give me good cover. The man from St. Louis was telling about somebody he knew way back when, somebody who'd been a heller in the old days, then got saved.

"Soon as he got the baptism of the Holy Spirit with evidence of speaking in tongues, he made the Lord a partner in his business. Called it Mason, Latham, and Lord— it was a coin business, gold Krugers, Latham never existed, and Lord, well—the Lord was a silent partner. The whole deal was nothing but a confidence game. Just what I'd always thought it was, the religion business, I mean. All smoke and mirrors, take my word for it. Holy moly, I *know*—I was born Catholic."

"Say what you will," the woman said.

"He thought he was sitting there with his ass in butter, but the Feds are no dopes . . . Stewie Mason's a guest of the government in the Federal Pen to this day. Been saved four or five times, maybe more. Maybe this time it will stick. Maybe, this time, he's really repented—"

The woman sounded startled. "Repainted?" she said.

"Re*pen*ted! Repented!" The man laughed. "Jeez—" he said.

There'd been a loud commotion—a siren, then a broken

sound like a rattling down of venetian blinds, huge ones. Then, quieter. A chuff of wind was all.

One of the feedyard men went to the door, opened it and looked out. "Sounded like a chopper to me," he said.

"Better close that!" Whitney yelled.

"Business is business. They're in it to make money," the woman said, "don't kid yourself."

Once the door was closed again, we could really appreciate how snug it was inside.

Whitney was busy putting out chips in bowls when the phone rang. He turned his back to us and leaned over the bottles, clapping a hand over his free ear to hear better. Then he stepped out from behind the bar, trailing the cord over his shoulder. "Anybody seen Bud—Bud Pearson?" he asked.

Nobody had.

An ad for orange juice was flashing over Whitney's head. Dumb, but full of color—a relief from traffic and weather. Sunshine juice . . . It was *really* dumb: a man and a woman side by side, plunging red and white candy-striped straws into oranges. Two screens, so four of everything. The man's straw had a normal gauge, and his orange was the usual tennis ball size, but the woman had a straw I'd never seen the likes of, the size of a muffler pipe, and she was trying to plunge it into this withered-up orange no fatter than a golf ball. She was mashing that poor orange pretty good. I remember it well because of what followed.

A news bulletin, and it had my full attention from the start. The first picture was angled in from the edge of a field. Bare, but furrowed, maybe just seeded. Littered with rubble now, big chunks of what must of been a good-sized jet. Parts of it were still showing red, though there was a bunch of trucks out there drowning the field, and one of them was slabbering foam over the wrecked cabin, lathering the whole deal with shaving cream, what it looked like.

The hippie who'd been playing pool by himself stepped up to the set for a closer look. He aimed his cue stick at the screen. His arm made a dicing motion. "Butcher's meat," he said, "you seen that?"

I missed it, whatever it was looked like chopped meat to him, but I recognized Mr. Titus talking to the county sheriff. The priest from Bounds was there, too, with a purple ribbon drooping from his neck. He was kneeling alongside of somebody on the ground. The camera zoomed in close as it could. It was a woman, gray-headed. She kept lifting one hand like she was swatting flies. Or maybe—couldn't blame her—trying to shoo the priest away.

"Hocus-pocus. He breathes on their eyes, see," the hippie explained. "They open on the other side."

Whitney was listening with one hand up, shading his eyes. "Why, that's Miss Wooten's place . . ."

"Looks like the end of the world to me," said the man from St. Louis.

Jack Henderson lifted his face from the paper. "What's going on?" he asked. He stared at the screen; his mouth hung open. "Will you lookit that—" He pointed to the priest. "He's basting them all in oil, the better to roast in hell. Catholic, now!"

Next thing they showed was the DFW airport. Planes landing and taking off, landing and taking off, same as every day. An airport official inside the terminal, pinned up against the wall by a reporter with a mike in his fist. "There were ninety-two passengers, and seven crew members on board," the official said. Didn't bat an eyelash. He was saying those numbers, but he was outside the saying of them. I can tell those things.

"Lord have mercy!" said the man from St. Louis. And I bet he was crossing himself, too.

The reporter on the screen shoved the mike forward again. "And how many casualties?" he asked.

"We're not for sure," the official said. The camera zoomed in closer. "There's been no word yet on casualties."

No word? If ever a barefaced lie! That really got next to me.

"How come you didn't hear it, Chip?" Whitney turned my way. "Big plane like that going down? You're not that far from the Wooten place."

Don't answer.

"Musta been all those dogs yapping," old Jack Henderson put in. "Yipping and yapping night and day, so what's the difference?"

Couldn't deal with it.

I don't play their games. I wiped my lips with the back of my hand and went on wiping. Just then came a big blare of light and noise—the electricity quit again. Somebody shouted, "Hell's bells!" and somebody knocked over couple of glasses trying to duck down under the bar. Didn't last but ten seconds. By the time everything was back to normal, I was reaching for my jacket. I stood up.

I wanted to see this shit for myself.

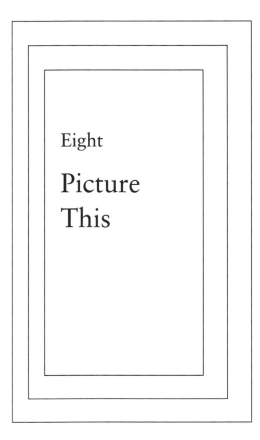

Eight

Picture
This

FRANCIE ALRED HERE. My name's Frances, but Francie's what I go by. I have to say right off that I never was a witness to the crash—unless visions count. That's my only piece of the picture for now. Fact is, I was way too late catching onto any facts. So let me just say a word about this dream I had, and the meeting afterwards that seemed like an echo to it, then I'll hand the story on.

The first thing about the dream was its coming when it

did, the night before the crash. I'd heard the wind, the whanging of the windmill, all night long, but I'd yet to step outside to realize how severe it was. Even that afternoon, when the electricity quit in town, I had no inkling of it, since I live on the Mastersons' property and they have their own generator. I knew it was cold but not how bitter. What I had most on my mind was this dream . . .

Soon as I woke, I knew it meant something. No saying what, though. I take all my dreams seriously. Most people here do, and anybody who lingers in the area usually gets in the habit of it. We don't have many distractions, so we attend to our dreams. Drop by the post office of a rainy afternoon and Glenna Wooten will try out her latest on you. And, goodness, Brother Pipes regularly broadcasts *his* every Sunday at nine on KVUZ, a station that pretty well covers the county! Dreams and weather are our main events. While I don't always talk about my dreams, I do mull over them. I'm not superstitious, don't claim to be psychic, and even though I was born and raised in the Bible Belt, I'm pretty much immune to religion. But I do believe in dreams, even if they seem to make no sense. I'm absolutely convinced that if you see a number in a dream, then you better bet on it, better put some money down on it. Dreams are like vapor trails. Vanishings: they point to real things. Things just beyond the rim of sight.

Like most dreams, mine was one thick snarl. Somewhere along in the middle of it, I heard a voice calling out, then something else happened—I can't for the life of me recall what—and then comes the part I do remember: seeing the old man. His hair was white. He was stooped over a burning barrel. It was bitter cold in the dream, as it was in waking fact. The old man was lighting up. Cigarette, I guessed, I couldn't see to tell; his face was bent so low it seemed to be grazing the flame. Then he straightened out, and, waving or blowing, sent a big billow of smoke in my direction. He was generating this just-incredible volume of smoke. I rushed at him, hollering at him to quit. Next frame: the old man leaning against the wall of a shed, smoking two cigarettes; they jutted out like tusks, one on either side of his nose. I asked him why: "Why two at once?" His answer—and here I recall every word: "It saves time." Then I woke up.

Sounds crazy, I know. My alarm was ringing—I'd forgotten to unset it for my day off. It could have been blasting away for some seconds before I reached out from under my warm covers and shut it off, so I probably had time on my mind. The alarm put me in mind of fire alarms, and the fire alarm very naturally suggested fire. So maybe it wasn't all that strange a dream . . . But then how to explain what came later in the day?

I was getting ready to leave the house when I heard a commotion outside. Sounded like it was coming from Chip Parker's place: a lot of yelping. Prowler? Couldn't tell, but decided to hug the house for a while. You can't fool dogs. So I tiptoed around, checking everything was tight, then sat myself down close to the phone. I was riding high on fear by then. Hearing a faint click, I froze to it, before realizing it was only the latch of my breath lifting. That's how intent I was. I waited maybe half an hour, sitting there in semi-dark, my ears cupped to the least stirring. There wasn't any noise to speak of while I waited. Except for the wind, which I'd gotten used to.

Until I heard a loud sigh. Seemed to be coming from close by, inside the house. The kitchen, I thought, and somehow my fear was played out by then—too long a wait, I guess, with nothing to show for it. So I got up to see. And, sure enough, there was the source of it: plaster sifting down from a gash in the ceiling. This lazy, whispery, sifting down, like loose flour. Nothing major but, again, puzzling. No point sweeping up yet; I'd give it time to settle, or develop, whatever it was.

We weren't on any fault line that I knew of. Besides—everything else in the kitchen looked solid, unshaken. I decided it best to steer clear of that particular room, though. Then the phone rang and I had to do an about-face; it's on the wall next to the stove.

Hard to tell who was calling at first, the line so full of static and the hum of other voices. Then it cleared: I recognized Whitney speaking. He was wanting to know whether I'd be willing to work this evening. He mentioned something about an accident and expecting a big bunch of people coming into town. "Coming from all over," he predicted. "Wait," I said, "back up a little—what's this about an accident?" He said, "Francie, where are you? What world are you *in?*" then told me what he knew. And I promised to be there. I'm not pinched, but I'm not so flush, either, that I can afford to sneeze at the extra income.

Soon as I stepped outside, I heard the dogs growling again. And now I thought I saw the cause of it: somebody trapped inside the fence, struggling to slip through.

I forgot all about my fear beforehand. A corner of his jacket was snagged on one of the barbs—he'd been thrashing around, making it worse. "Hold it!" I shouted as I moved towards him. "Let me help you—"

One glance told me he'd been through something drastic. He was wearing only half a tie. No shoes. There was a smudge on one cheek, or some skin barked off of it. He'd been part of the accident Whitney had been talking about, I felt sure.

He stared at me with the blankest eyes I've ever seen. Eyes crusted with some muck—old tears, maybe. "How about if you try slipping out of your jacket? See—" I showed him how to stoop to the level of the wire, to pull out one arm at a time, slowly, with me holding the sleeve taut. "There you go." I lifted the jacket free and clear. Only a small rip that I could see, one easily mended. I handed the jacket back to him. He turned the thing over, lining side out, inspecting it; his hands moved like crabs, fingers crawling along the seams, fluttering into the deep sockets of the armholes, baffled. Like he'd never seen armholes before. I guess if you hadn't—to a Martian, for instance—they'd look pretty strange. He was no Martian, though. It was biting cold but, try as I might, I couldn't persuade him to put his arms back in. He turned to me and asked, perfectly serious, "What is the business you are in?"

I gave a little hoot to that. What a question! It's a good one: what business *am* I in? This happens to be one I've been putting to myself a lot lately, but he went right on asking things without waiting for anything from me. "Are you from Lübeck?" was next.

I heard him, all right—it sounded like "Loobeck," but for a second I thought he meant Lubbock. Anybody here would.

"Lubbock?" I answered. "No, why? Are you?" That was only to be saying something. I knew he wasn't.

He took off without answering—he'd spotted the gate and was headed for it. I argued with him to hold it for a minute. Words just seemed to lose themselves in the air, though, so I ran to catch up with him. He was going at a clip and it was all I could do to keep alongside. Once, when he started to pitch forward, I reached out and grabbed his arm, but he twisted himself away. That cautioned me about getting forward with a stranger. I kept on talking, didn't matter what, anything to keep him from slipping away. He made a remark to the ground: "Some pisk!" I didn't know what that meant, but I knew he meant me. His walk was wobbly, like he had one foot in a furrow.

Even so, he was too fast for me. He kept on spurting ahead, I kept on pursuing. The wind was mean, cutting, but I was in a fizz—I no longer felt it.

I didn't notice the woman till I was practically on top of her, my focus so set and centered on the old man. I guess she'd been crouched all that time, poking through a patch of shinnery, as she was when I came up to her. "Did you see an old man passing this way?" I hailed her. She must have.

"What?" She raised herself, glancing east and west. Seemed to be having some difficulty locating me. I asked again.

"Never met the guy," she said. "What's the hurry?"

"Explain later," I promised. "You lose something?"

"My keys." She looked very worried. "I've got everything on the one ring. Stupid! Can't think where I dropped them . . ."

"I'll be back," I said. I meant to be. I kept on moving, though, never breaking my stride. Don't know why, but I felt the old man was my first responsibility.

In fact, I lost sight of him long before giving up. Only on my way back, registering the cold afresh, thinking on the uselessness of my chase, did I recall the woman looking for her keys. She'd been in city dress and she hadn't been wearing shoes—it only struck me then—she'd been one of them.

But she, too, had vanished.

I was winded. All I could do was beat a retreat to the house and ring up the sheriff's office. I was scanning the horizon one last time before stepping inside when a piece of paper blew right up to me as if addressed and flattened against my shin. I peeled it off: a scrap of newspaper from somewhere—words broken off—nothing whole on it. None of this made sense. Time to quit! I'd make my phone call to the sheriff, catch my breath, then haul myself over to Tick Tock Lounge.

TWO

Nine

Voices

"ANYBODY ELSE from Golden Tours?" I could hear somebody with a bullhorn calling. "We've got a van waiting. Follow my voice—your van is waiting . . ." I wasn't dreaming, that's what I heard.

Looked like every kind of contraption on wheels had pulled up by the time I actually started on back to the house. Ambulance, flatbed truck, closed van, police cruiser. I'd seen an empty tractor trailer for carting who-knew-what stationed behind my shed. Add to that, the cars and vans parked every whichway between the house and the field, stacked up onto my lawn, even. A police officer from out of town was standing in the middle of my tomato patch, head tucked into one of those portable phones. He was discussing the crash, and he was talking in code, nothing I could follow. Then my ears pricked up. "It bought the farm," he said. "You should see it. It really bought the farm. Half a section, I'd say."

That roused me. They'd occupied, no disputing that, but they hadn't bought it yet!

I was so done-in, filthy with tiredness. Too tired to go to my own funeral, as they say. Too many mixed feelings too fast.

Even after I stepped inside and shut the door on them, I could still hear the rescuers, still see the scene in my mind's eye. The foam trucks had arrived a while back. They'd started out in one spot, covering the big pieces of wreckage, the last shreds of smoke, blanketing even the puddles where oil had seeped. They'd "neutralized" the field—I'd heard the firemen say so. Another one said "sealing." Or maybe "sealant," my hearing's not what it was. Anyway, the ground was all lathered up. What those chemicals would do to the soil was something I didn't want to think about.

There'd be no crop from it this year.

Times I want to just run—tear up my roots and run. This was one of those times. The hail-out last year was another. I'd given Troy my word, though, and I knew I wouldn't go back on it, come hell or high water. And that was what I had—hell *and* high water. But I'd promised

Troy that I'd hold on to the land long as I lived for the sake of the kids. I knew *they* didn't want it, and the grandkids wouldn't, but I was bound by my word to hang on. And, most times, I wanted nothing more than to be bound. Tear up your roots, your sworn promises, and you'll scatter in the first gust—that was the way of things. Look what was happening in the big cities, all you had to do was look around.

Then I thought about how nobody would want to buy the field after this. My next thought was nothing to be proud of, either. It was: count your blessings. Be glad it missed the house. Be glad it missed the set-aside. Be glad it missed the stubble field—imagine if it hadn't!

But I was too tired to feel anything by then.

I was standing in the hallway all this while and what I saw next gave me a start. Must of been some kind of afterimage or something, some trick of tired sight. Seemed to me the fridge door was open, somebody standing there, his back to me, half-blotting out its light. He was studying the food situation, hunting down a bedtime snack—Troy's old habit. I thought I heard him speak, too, without ever once turning round. "I'm home," he said, but his voice was just a blowing sound, low, soft, so low-spoken, "ho-ohm"—no body to it at all.

The fridge door was shut tight when I got to it.

I was hollow of a sudden, faint. I hadn't ever gotten around to eating supper, so no wonder. I needed something to keep up my strength. When I turned on the stove, the gas jet bloomed out like a circle of blue crocus—it startled me. Almost forgotten that fire could be so tame. So pretty. I started off with soup and toast, then, still feeling shaky—but no more voices or visions now—I fried an egg and perked that up with white pepper and a side serving of pickled beets. Heartless? Maybe so. I ended with a slice of Alma Hudson's lemon pie. Kept telling myself that I needed energy, that food would steady me, but even after I was full, I felt as shaky as before.

It was the same thing I'd done after Troy's funeral. The neighbors urged me to it, of course, heaping my plate with this and that, and all but raising my fork for me. I commenced eating and kept at it till I was well stuffed. Trying to remind myself that I was still alive. Same thing, then and now.

When I was done eating, I was still tired and still unready for sleep, so I washed and stacked the dishes. Soaking my hands in dishwater, after all that chill outside, felt right good to me, but I needed something else to busy me after the dishes were done. What would that be?

I decided to dust in the parlor. It was crazy, but it helped. Took my mind off other things. I steered well clear of the windows. I did the whatnot and most of the bric-a-brac in it, then the end tables on either side of the couch, then the piano. Then I turned to the framed photographs top of the piano. Whole row of pictures telling me who I'd been. The wedding ones were biggest. I stood there holding the one of Troy and me up to the lamplight and staring hard like I'd never laid eyes on us before. Then I took in the whole picture: it's a double: Troy and me, his brother Wayne and Anna. We couldn't afford but the one wedding in those days. There we were in our new-bought finery, you could see how unaccustomed. Me and Anna are seated, the grooms (both passed on now) flanking us like dark pillars. I'm showing off my new ring, my fingers rayed out to display it. Nothing to brag on, but I was proud of its three bright stones. They come out like little lead specks in the picture, though. I'm in a white linen summer dress with a shawl collar. Can't see what shoes— my legs only go up to the knees. Anna's wearing all lace with a high neck and princess sleeves. Must of been hot, but she doesn't show it. The men are dark-suited and stiff, close-lipped, grim. Like their teeth are clamping down on the word "forever"—starting to get the savor of it. Look again: not a one of us is smiling.

So different from the kids at their weddings, all wide-lipped, laughing or saying "cheese" for the camera. "Cheese" or "whiskey," lighthearted. Theirs are all in color; ours black and white, for hard choices. For us marriage meant forever. Theirs are for right now, so long as it pleases. The difference shows—Mike already on his second go-round, Audry quarreling with Norbert, talking of a "trial separation," though they happened to be together as of last week. Al was sticking; they'd only been married a few years, him and Mary. No saying how long that would last. It's a whole new world now, I reminded myself for the umpteenth time, but I couldn't agree that new meant better.

After dusting, I might of started in vacuuming, if I hadn't felt ready to drop on the spot. So, at last, I let myself stretch out on the couch. My spare blankets were outside—in use—and I had barely enough energy to fetch a couple of coats from the closet to cover myself with. No strength to make my way upstairs to a real bed, just

enough energy left to turn out the lights. It was shadowy
with the lights out, but not dark.

Laying there on the couch, away from the press of people, the chill crept deep into my bones again. All done-in
. . . yet I couldn't fall asleep. My eyes refused to close, I
was too balled-up inside. I'd always thought of my house
as a capsule, walled off from cold and pain. Even during
the dust bowl days, no matter the howling outside, I'd
kept steady and gone around stuffing damp towels and
washcloths under the door and into the window seams
until I felt we were sealed safely in. Funnel clouds, lightning, hail—I still thought the same thing. But this crash
had gotten to me. Felt like it split the roof wide open. I
could hear the wind close at hand and, even with the windows closed, a never-ending commotion from the field.

There were bullhorns, sirens blaring, choppers chop-
ping, car motors gunning in the cold. I could make out
each separate sound and map its position. It's my land,
after all, nobody living knows it like I do. I know it by
inches.

I even thought I could hear them hacking and sawing
away at the passenger cabin. It was cool enough now to
start. With my right mind, I knew I was too far off to hear
them if they really had started, but I'd seen the rescue crew
laying out their tools, so I knew what kind of work lay
ahead. There were hatchets, big ones—they had no need
of mine—and cutting torches. Chisels and harness cutters.
Ladders, ropes, pliers, crowbars. And saws—electric-pow-
ered, double-bladed. They called them "rescue saws."
They'd asked to use my shed as a temporary morgue.

The things I'd witnessed today—a whole world in

pieces! I pictured Troy at my side, helpmeet, how I wished he were here to help me through this, all the while knowing he wouldn't of had the strength for it. Not in his last years, and maybe not for years before that when he must of been failing and trying to hide it.

He'd been falling for months. Always some excuse: his shoes not fitting right—they didn't *make* shoes to fit properly anymore, an uneven step that tripped him up, hiccups, heart cough, a patch of floor I'd overwaxed—till he fell from his chair, fell from his bed, and we knew it was no accidental thing, it was more like the earth was drawing him down. He fought it. I think he knew well what it was.

How I fussed and schemed for his last birthday! Roused myself at the crack of dawn, even though it was a Sunday, to lay out the new sweater I'd knitted for him and his favorite kind of cake, apple spice, fresh baked. And he pushed it all away from him. Wouldn't even *try* on the sweater, wouldn't touch the cake. Didn't say ten words to me all that morning.

Al was visiting at the time, all three of us sitting together at the table, the silence so thick you could taste it. Finally, I turned to Al. "Ask your father what he wants," I said, " 'cause I don't know anymore. Nothing I make for him." So Al blurted out: "What's eating you, Pa? What is it you want?"

Troy answered right away, didn't take a minute to think it over. "Everything," he said. That was his last birthday. He knew.

I was thinking back on that birthday for a reason, asking what it was those passengers wanted, and knowing the answer was: everything. Everything! Who wants less? I saw the plane again, speeding down, down to nothing, saw Troy again, stumbling— Sat up sharp then, tossing my head from side to side, trying to shake off what I'd seen. It was no dream, I was still awake, too weighted with eating, I thought, eating and other things, to drift off.

When I stretched out again, I could hear the wind, still battering away. I saw Jim Titus being blown backwards by the wind. That wasn't how it was, so I thought maybe I'm starting to dream now, maybe I'm drowsing at last. Strange . . . for I was growing heavier by the minute, so swollen with holding in . . . I could hear old Dr. Porter saying, "You've got to dilate one more inch," but I couldn't take it anymore and I cried back, "This is it—as far as I go!" And Troy's there standing side of my bed. "Hon . . ."—he's bending close—"hear what the doctor says" and he holds to his chest a present a basket something red. Cherries of all things darkly red

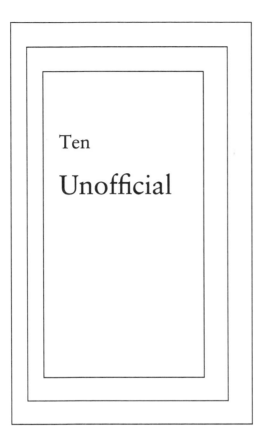

Ten

Unofficial

I STOPPED back at the house to look in on my dogs and feed them. The Blue Heelers were on the prod, jumpy as could be, but there wasn't a one of them, breed or no breed, who hadn't picked up on something. They all knew there'd been one hell of a ruckus nearby and that Buck hadn't come back with me.

And then I split. I recalled Whitney saying as I was leaving the lounge, "I wouldn't mess with it, Chip, if I was you. They'll close off the area first thing." I knew he was probably right, but I had to see for myself.

All along the sides of the road leading to the Wooten place, for a good quarter of a mile, they'd set down flares. But the field itself—you'd have to be blind to miss it. Lights on tripods everywhere, camera floodlights with their own portable generators. Police barricades, to keep anybody unofficial out. Bunch of officers propped up by those boards.

"Sorry, son, this is out of bounds to visitors," is the friendliest greeting I got. "But I'm *in* Bounds," I said, trying to make a joke of it. "Born and raised here—never have been out." He wasn't smiling. "You know what I'm talking about," he said, "don't get smart-mouthed." He was nobody I'd ever seen before. Must of come from Hardesty or farther yet. "I mean unofficial," he said, "that's what you are." I offered to let him use some of my dogs. "They're good trackers," I let him know, "might be somebody got away or something." No thank you very much, was his answer to that—they had their own dogs for tracking if they needed them. I'd heard about rescue dogs going into action with two-way transistor radios latched onto their harnesses, special dogs taught to bark into microphones when they came on whatever it was they were trained to look out for. My dogs are plenty smart, but none of that. So I backed off.

I knew my way around better than they could. So I prowled around the back road that runs between the Wooten set-aside and Darrel Richardson's field. And, sure enough, I spied my opening and snuck in easy. What was left of the passenger cabin and some parked vans gave me good cover. Plus, there was this curtain of smoke between me and the lighted area of the field. I crept along, following the wreckage trail. The soles of my boots felt paper thin, crunching. Too much metal underfoot, everything cut and cutting. Like a great big can opener had run over the ground, going berserk. Then there was jet fuel seeping along or squishing out of the mud. And foam. Thorny or boggy, didn't know which was worse, there was no ground you could trust. Slab of wing up ahead, broken off, bent at the tip, aluminum skin crumpled up like real skin. I was stepping careful, close to it, when it started to hum and sizzle like bacon on a fry pan. Or a swarm of bees—

Jumped clear of it—you bet, quick! The sound was coming from some shredded wires in the wing. Could be stepping on mines, I thought, most anything could explode yet, so I veered away sharp from it, moving quick as I could.

Spotted something bright out behind the shed—bright in its own light. I went after it. Suitcase ripped wide open, what it was. Stuff scattered all over—clothes—bright clean new ones. Nighties, they call them, naughty nighties. They were slinky—I stooped to pick up one of them and let it go. It was slimy. Gross!

Thought I saw a gold coin. Too good to be true, it was only a cigar, fancy kind, the foil ring had caught my eye. Turned out to be sopping wet, so I let it go.

I turned around back of the shed. Noticed a lady sitting there, strapped to her chair, and went up as close as I could. She might of been just resting there—except for the torched hair and a wide-open look of astonishment in her blue eyes. The chair was right side up, but stowed at a crazy angle. She'd dressed for this—frilly blouse, pink fingernails—a party wilder than planned.

It was weird—horrorshow terrific. I felt sorry for her, sure, but—hey!—hey, I didn't do it. I spotted a peaked blue cap with gold braid. That was something I really wanted to pick up, but knew the airline officials would be looking for it first thing, they'd know it was missing.

Anyhoo—then I saw something even better.

A hand. I'm flipping out. A man's hand, all there is to it. Size of my own, about. Chopped off, neat, at the wrist. Weird! I stoop down close to make sure, my mind whizzing along at this dizzy speed: ninetysome passengers and each of them has, what, three-hundred-sixty bones—heard that someplace—so ninety times three hundred is zero times zero is zero times nine times anything is zero . . . six times nine is fifty-four four carry the five three times nine is twenty-seven plus five that's thirty-two—thirty-two-thousand-four-hundred bones! A *heap* of bones, one big bundle of sticks spewed out over the field. And say they broke off between the joints every whichwhere in between, billions and zillions of bits in between what I'm thinking my hand sliding down for his hand tucking it a little cold a little clammy into my hip pocket, my right-hand loose-change pocket. Keep going. Doing okay, great, hey—everything cool, everything interesting, so *interesting,* nothing getting to me as I walk along sort of blinkered now sort of strolling-through scouting along whatever turns up next diamond ring coke maybe smugglers' stash when my hand goes back to my pocket forgetting for a sec and—yow!—which hand is

which? Some other mouth not mine starts up. I'm so
spaced. Howling—I can hear it—me? That me? Yowling
—like a bitch in heat! Can't be me! Split—gotta split— So
I start running—can't see anything it's a blur—gotta get
outta here—gotta get out—but it's hard-going shredded
metal, filaments—the word comes to me *filaments* hooks
everywhere trying to catch—and catching—a tall thorn
in my foot. And worse—worse yet—that hard hand jounc-
ing— Five dead fingers hooked to my hip! And somebody
else yelling, grabbing ahold of my hair by the root—

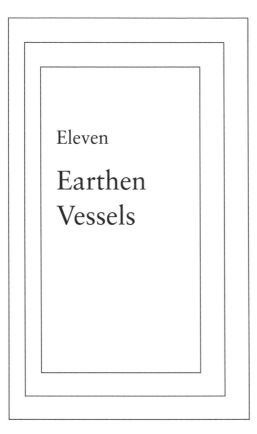

Eleven

Earthen Vessels

DO NOT BE AFRAID of those who kill the body but cannot kill the soul. A little darkness would have been soothing. Instead, they'd made a circle around the wrecked passenger cabin, stringing up klieg lamps. Klieg, or strobe—like stage lights—garish, unreal-making. *Do not be afraid . . .* This would be it: the final act. They were using acetylene torches on the cabin now, going in for the last of the bodies. Human cargo. I had to face away for a moment, lean against the hood of a car. The moment passed; I tried to pick up the passage where I'd left off. *Are not two sparrows sold for a small coin? Yet not one of them falls to the ground without your Father's knowledge*—guess my head wasn't buried deeply enough in the text. I could still see a corona of light over the page's rim, gibbering shadows moving across the light. One shadow separated out from the rest, grew dimensional, grew bright. It was no one I recognized. He was resolutely heading my way.

I guess he took my glance as a greeting, because he started up right away.

"You're the priest, right?" I nodded. He introduced himself—a reporter, I forget which paper. I realized then that he'd introduced himself earlier. But that had been hours before. It had been a long night.

"You've"—he fished around for the right word—"been working with the dying, I noticed. 'Extreme unction'— that what you call it?"

"Used to call it. I've been anointing them, yes." I didn't want to get into a long discussion. He wasn't content to leave it at that, though.

"You see," he persisted, "and this is strictly off the record, for my own benefit—but I can't understand what you've been doing. I can't help noticing that you've not been very discriminating. Between ourselves, Father, haven't you been anointing everybody? I mean, but *everybody?*"

He didn't wait for an answer.

"Saints and sinners. Moslems. Jews. Mormons? Atheists, too, I bet."

"Would you have me take a census first?" I asked.

He rubbed at something on his sleeve. "So it's for consolation," he said. "Just kindness."

"Kindness?" The word was one of those warm fuzzies I didn't much trust. "It isn't social work I've been up to."

"I don't understand," he said.

How to even begin to explain? Did *I* understand it? Officially, only the baptized, the catechized, the prepared, the shriven, were really blessed by such a gesture, only for these was the anointing a sacrament. For others, it was neither sacrament nor sacramental. "Well, but look . . ." I said, and ground to a halt.

"What would the Pope have to say about it?"

"The Pope?" I must have sighed. This wasn't the place . . . How could he not see that?

Maybe he did, though. "Sorry," he said, "it's my job to ask questions. Gets to be a habit, I'm afraid, even when I'm off the job."

He really wanted to know. I tried to think, but it's hard to find the right language for someone who isn't steeped in the traditions. Lots of things are second nature to us. I gave it one more stab. "For a Catholic," I said, "a Catholic who's spiritually prepared for it, the anointing is full of meaning—layer after layer of meaning. For others, this wouldn't be the case. But I can't tell who's who in a situation like the one we've got. *Obviously.*" I tried to make clear how the anointing, and the absolution that went with it, were conditional, how we do it, just in case, when we don't know the facts of the case. Better to err on the side of lavishness if you don't know—that's what we'd been taught.

And that, apparently, cleared me with the Pope. He didn't ask me what I, personally, thought. They never do —assuming that the Pope does all our thinking for us. What did I think? Right then? To be honest? I saw only the denominations of pain: Burns, Breaks, Bleeds. And one Lord of Suffering over all.

"One last question, Father?"

"Okay," I agreed. But I made him promise it would be the last.

"Let me check that I've got this straight. What I'm hearing is: in most cases, going by the book, the anointing doesn't stick. Doesn't *take*. Like an inoculation that doesn't take. You said 'conditional,' right? Only conditional. So . . . if they don't meet the conditions—say they're not Catholic, or they *are* Catholic but not in the right condition to receive it, then it doesn't work. So it's mostly—don't misunderstand me, Father, I don't mean to be disrespectful—but if you look at it that way, then it's got to be, in a lot of cases, just wasted oil and a wistful prayer—"

"Not wasted, no," I hastened to reply. "Not wistful." What, then? There was a gap in the rubrics, something unexplained. He stared at me fixedly, waiting. I had to say something, so I temporized: "Look, I wouldn't put it that starkly. If you're really interested, swing by the church sometime, and we'll sit down and have a long talk about it. I'd welcome that. Only, not tonight. Okay?"

"Got news for you. It's morning, Father."

So it was. You could see an opening in the grayness to the east, some long clouds trailing like streamers. "We'll talk again sometime," I promised, "if you're interested."

"You bet. Appreciate it," he said. "Enjoyed visiting with you." He started to walk off briskly, then turned, put his finger to his lips. "Strictly confidential!" he said loudly.

Gazing out over the field, I could see ribbons of gauze fluttering in the rubble. Smoke, thin and forceless now, drifted over the ground, clinging low. The rescue squad was still sawing away at the crumpled cabin wall. Except for the methodical grinding of metal on metal, relative quiet reigned: there were no more shouts or cries. The dying and the injured had been evacuated first. Then the walk-aways. Then the dead—except for those trapped in the cabin—my thoughts kept on circling back to them.

So there it was: a new day. The yellowing, too-cheerful light grated me. I'd started out wearing my coat, the air temperature close to freezing, but, as the evening wore on, I'd grown strangely warm. Shivering into warmth, maybe.

Told myself I ought to be praying. Words came to mind, a long drumroll of words . . . *afflicted, but not constrained . . . struck down, but not destroyed* . . . Only one phrase resonated for me—*earthen vessels.*

Seemed like only a bare couple of minutes, for I'd only begun to catch my breath before I spied someone else headed towards me. Turned out to be a deputy sheriff from Hardesty I'd had dealings with before. Landrum, I think his name is—I couldn't get his badge into focus to be sure. "Got a case for you, Father," he said.

"What kind of case?"

"Souvenir hunter, I guess you'd call it."

Took me a minute, making sense of that. "You mean people gather up pieces for fun?" I asked.

"You'd be surprised," he said. "All kinds of fun in this

world. And looting, it's a regular business. It's also a crime, destroying evidence at the scene of an accident. This young fellow we caught—you figure this one out—had a hand in his pocket."

"So?" I didn't get it.

"Somebody else's hand—a piece of the evidence, see? Maybe you could speak to him, Father. We can't seem to get through to him. He's been bawling nonstop, like a lost infant. Dry tears—the worst kind. He's in big trouble."

"*That* him?" I was surprised when it turned out to be Chip Parker. Last person in the world I would have expected. The bawling part, I mean. Couldn't ever imagine Chip showing emotion in public. It wasn't in character, and he'd worked hard to establish his character—flinty, indifferent—choosing to spend more time in the company of dogs than people.

If he'd been overcome with emotion before, it was well past by the time I got to him. They'd roughed him up: he looked chalky, shaken, his lower lip cracked, one cheek swollen and striped. I thought I could read the print of a hand in those stripes, of fingers outstretched. I asked that we be allowed to talk in private.

He'd been "stressed-out, freaked-out," was how Chip explained it. Only hours before, he'd had to put one of his dogs to sleep. Once he learned of the crash, he'd ventured out to the site to see what was what, and all the carnage "got to him." Not very informative, and I wasn't sure whether the dog's death or the human carnage had hit him hardest. Nothing he said did much to explain why he'd chosen to appropriate another man's hand, but Chip

quickly lapsed into wordlessness and I knew it was hopeless to press for more. Something claps shut in him.

Afterwards, I did my best to embellish the story for the
arresting officer. I carried on quite a bit with the little I
knew, surprising myself at it. Told him how Chip had
been as law-abiding as the next citizen before this incident. No record that I was aware of, but I expected he'd
check that out for himself. And then I handed on a little of
his history, how he'd been raised by his only known kin,
an elderly bachelor uncle, an unsociable man—or maybe a
little deaf—anyhow, a man disinclined to make conversation. How Chip had grown up in all that silence, on his
own, pretty much foraging for himself. And how—this
struck me as important now—there'd been two of them—
he'd been one of a set, a twin, his brother crushed in a
baling accident when the boys were toddlers. I didn't
know exactly how old Chip would have been at that time,
but I knew it was very young. I recalled what I'd heard
from others in town—that Chip had been earning his own
keep since he turned seven, killing rats at so much a head
and, later, rabbits. Collecting hangers and selling them to
the cleaners, things like that. He wasn't Catholic, but he'd
done odd jobs in my parish; his story was well known in
Bounds.

About the twin part, it occurred to me afterwards, it's
as though he's been running away from somebody all of
his life, and that somebody might be a full half of himself.
He wasn't "all there," in the judgment of most people in
town. I hadn't mentioned that.

"We'll release him this time on your say-so," the officer
granted after I was done making what case I could. "But

not the next time. Make sure he understands that. He likes to act deaf, I think. Tell him we've got our eye on him, got all the vital statistics. Tell him to start marching. Out *this* way"—pointing to an opening in the barricades—"not the way he came. No funny business."

I was whipped. Unstrung. I stood on after Chip left, rocking a little on my feet, my eyes half-closed, unable to quit the spot. The field was quiet, near empty now. Only shadows, revenants, moved—a dreamlike figure, in a silver bodysuit and helmet, gently poking a pile of ash with a long steel rod. The sun drifted out, partway, from behind a cloud; the widening light was grating to eyes as tired as mine, an obscene gilding of a scene of unspeakable horror. My eyes were painfully dry. Tears would have helped, would have been cleansing, but no tears were forthcoming. When the sun broke free of the cloud, I realized that it was going to be a beautiful day. Yet, wherever I looked, there was a smudge, a shadow, an afterimage, as if I'd been staring too long at the sun.

It was already after seven. Too late to make my usual early morning Mass. Given the circumstances, my daily communicants would understand. I had no idea what I was waiting around for, but I wasn't yet ready to quit the field. Too tired to move. So I lingered, useless, still upright though half-asleep, trying to keep my eyelids pried apart —straining. Images flared up, like dreaming on my feet. Same scene: I'm gazing out. Near the ruined passenger cabin, there's a peaceful lagoon of seeped kerosene. Oily gleams. There's ash still sifting through the air and, in the smoldering rubble, a hand. A hand rises, the bones incandescent, the fingers—wicks, little spouts of flame at each fingertip . . .

"Can you pray like that?"

"What?" I felt myself pitching forward—jolting awake. "How do you mean?"

"Like you were doing just now—eyes closed, standing up. Looking like you're about to keel over?"

It was one of the nurses. She held out a plastic cup to me: steaming. Afraid I'd spill it—one knee was quaking and I didn't feel steady at all—I reached for it with both hands.

Twelve

Tracking

"DEE O BEE?" the officer said.

"*What?* What did you say?" The daughter of the man they were searching for sounded angry, close to tears. The least little thing touched her off. She'd survived the crash —so had her father, to hear tell—then she'd lost him. Her left hand was heavily bandaged but she kept on forgetting, trying to smooth her hair with it. It was one big ball of bandage, like a boxer's mitt. Aside from that, her face was a little scratched, that's all. Not much, considering.

"Date of birth?" the officer explained.

"Oh, hell, I can't."

"Well, *about* then. Give us an about."

They went on that way with height, weight, hair color. Somewhere along in there I realized they were talking about the old man I'd run into, the one with the smudge on his cheek and only half a tie. I spoke up then, and the daughter brightened. "That's him," she said, "definitely." So I invited her into the house to help pass the time while she was waiting.

Before we took off, the officer wanted to know if she had any photos with her. She fumbled in her purse for one, wedging it open with her mitt and poking around with her good hand till she found something. She passed it to me first, and I nodded, "the same." Gray face, smudge of hair, bitter line of lip, thin as a thread. A man of years, unpleased by growing old. Not much help in a photograph like that, I thought; could of been Troy, my father, anyone. The officer pocketed the thing without comment, then handed around the notice he'd been drafting for a final check. Within hours, you'd see it on the walls of most public buildings in town. I'd be tacking one up in the post office if he stayed missing till tomorrow.

ALZHEIMER'S VICTIM
MISSING
SIMCHA WEISS

DESCRIPTION: 5'6" medium weight, 79 years old, gray-haired, brown eyes, suffers from diabetes and memory-robbing Alzheimer's. Known to be

wearing a gray suit, white shirt, blue
tie. Wears glasses for reading.

LAST SEEN: Bounds, Texas, survivor of
an air crash. He may have accepted a
ride out of the area. Though able to
carry on a limited conversation, Mr.
Weiss would not know his way home.
Born in Germany, he has lived most
of his adult life in New York City. He
speaks with an accent.

IF SEEN PLEASE CONTACT . . .

Then the sheriff's number was listed. And **URGENT** in
big bold letters after that.

We settled at the kitchen table, the daughter and me.
There wasn't a whole lot between us, nothing in common,
really, but the crash. That didn't give us much to go on.
She said her name was Rachel, and I said call me Glenna.
She told me her father's name was "Simcha," but I'd read
the notice and already knew that. The name "Simcha,"
she said tearfully, meant "Joy." A man named Joy! Never
in my life have I heard of a man with a name such as that
—one or two girls, yes, but of course I didn't say so. On
the way, I tried to distract her by showing off my vegeta-
ble garden-to-be, my tomatoes and early-bird peppers in
cups on the windowsill, but she only mumbled some be-
ing-polite sounds like "mmm" and "mm-hmm" and I
knew her thoughts were elsewhere. She'd noticed the sun-
dial before that, even paused to read the inscription on it:
I COUNT NONE BUT SUNNY HOURS, mouthing the words in won-

derment. She's still in a daze, I thought, urging her on into the kitchen.

Inside, I warmed up two thick slices of my apple cake and brewed a fresh pot of coffee. She pecked at the cake and took maybe two sips of the coffee, dawdling until it was surely chilled. True, she had only one hand with that big mitt of hers. I offered to hot up her cup for her. "Better not, thanks," she said; she didn't know how caffeine combined with her pain medication. I'd resolved to say nothing more of the crash unless she brought it up, and that didn't leave us a whole lot else to talk about.

Still—I'd been upholding my end of the conversation with precious little to work with, blatting on about Bounds and the postal business, if only to keep something going, when she started to weep, these strangled, clotted sounds that stopped me cold. I reached over, patted her good hand, and waited for words. A minute or two and they came—"Everything's slipping away from him"—in a rush.

"Wasn't so long ago he could still explain how he felt trying to recall the names of things and failing. 'Like trying to count the doors in a dream,' he said. Now he can't explain anything. Like, he used to say: 'We Jews are in the business of remembering.' When I was growing up, I didn't want to hear about it, about his growing up Jewish in Berlin. I was sick of being reminded forever. Now I *want* to know and he can't tell me. He was such an intelligent man. A brilliant man—"

"Is—*is*," I reminded her. "I saw him. He was quick, let me tell you. But not so quick that they won't be able to catch up with him."

"You don't know how humiliating it is." She was still harping on his forgetfulness. "All the time I've spent waiting at the doors of men's rooms, not knowing if he's going to come out. Standing there and everybody noticing . . .

"The thing is, in a crazy way, he's still on top of certain things. Like he didn't want to fly today, he didn't trust the weather. Looking back, knowing what I do now, that showed a lot of good sense. I wish I'd heeded him, but I couldn't see it then. He did everything he could to dissuade me. He even tried to make out he'd been reading his obituary—his own obituary!—in the paper. Can you imagine? He rattled the newspaper in my face until I agreed to read it."

"Well, then?" That sounded pretty purposeful to me.

"And I did, and I laughed at him. There was no similarity at all between the man who'd died and Pop, no possible resemblance. Pop wasn't laughing along with me, so I tried to reason with him. 'Look,' I said, 'he's got an Oriental name—see—' It was Dan Ban Phang, or something. Sounded like somebody banging pots and pans—you know?—one of those names. That didn't stop Pop, though. He pointed to the man's picture and I had to laugh. 'So he's got glasses, big deal, you both wear glasses! You don't look a bit like him. The man's not even Jewish, Pop. He's Chinese—' He jabbed at the paper again, so I scanned the article, trying to find the least shred of sense in it, the least connection with my father. Couldn't find a thing. But I'd gotten one thing wrong, so I corrected myself. 'Okay, he's Vietnamese,' I said. 'So? You know anybody Vietnamese? Even one person? He comes from a whole other world!' Then Pop pushed his chair away from

the table, stamped to his feet. I knew he was really angry. Actually hurt. 'What am I—*tata* or *schmatte?*' he said."
The daughter glanced up then, taking me in, maybe for the first time. "Don't know why I'm running on like this," she said. "I keep forgetting you wouldn't understand. 'Am I *tata* or *schmatte?*' means: 'Am I a father or a rag?' " She searched my face for my reading of that. I didn't know what she wanted me to do, laugh or cry, had no idea what sort of face I was supposed to give back to her. Must of just looked muddled. "Guess that's lost in translation," she said. "Anyway, the thing is—I knew then that he remembered he was my father. At least . . . as long as he was saying it, he remembered. Most of the time now he doesn't have a clue . . ."

"Use the napkin," I suggested, supposing it was a hanky she was after. She'd started sniffling and poking around in her purse. She shook her head, no, it was something else—a pillbox—she wanted. One of those long ones that mean business. She popped it open with one hand and pointed out seven dividers, one for each day of the week—she'd laid out a whole week's worth of medication before the flight. "He needs these." She fingered the different colors. "The little one is the most important. He's a whole day late on everything."

"He'll come round," I promised. "You'll see." She made a sound—of air trapped behind teeth. I knew then how desperate she was. "You'll see," I repeated. "Take my word for it. I've lived a lot longer than you."

Might as well of been talking to the air.

"Sometimes," she went on, "he seems like less than one person. Sometimes like a whole crowd in one. You know?

I haven't heard him call me by my name in—don't know how long. Has he forgotten that, too? What about his own name? Will that be next? I don't dare to put him to the test. When he signs a check, I can tell he's not really writing. He's drawing a picture of his name, that's all, and that picture's going to be the next thing to go—"

"You have children?" I asked, hoping a change of subject might perk things up.

"Daughter"—she sighed—"and she's going through a very difficult adolescence. So I'm pulled—torn—in two different directions."

"Don't I know it!" I said. "We call them 'the taffy years.' " No way of telling whether she heard me or not, but I persisted. "Caught between the generations— stretched near to breaking between them. Like taffy." I was making a serious point, I wanted her to know that. "Anybody my age—we've been there."

Then I heard gravel churning on the front drive and I thought *none too soon* . . . My welcome to Matt Mc-Kee, our deputy sheriff, was warm and hearty—I couldn't help showing my relief. "*Almost* good news," he said; he was expecting it soon, and had come to fetch the daughter.

There'd been a couple of leads. A motorist passing by a salvage yard north of the city had spotted an old man standing and staring. " 'Looking kinda lost' was his impression." By the time the motorist picked up the *Alzheimer's Victim Missing* bulletin at a gas station fifteen miles down the road, it was too late to turn back, but the man had paused to place a call to the sheriff's office, and Matt had gone out to look. He found the place deserted.

There'd been a second sighting on Longview and Hale; it hadn't matched the first, and hadn't led to anything, either. But Matt thought it best to have the daughter close at hand for when the next call came in.

She all but leapt to her feet, so eager to be gone. Thanked me in a big voice and asked where she could freshen up, her mind already on the next thing.

I wanted to press Matt for more details while she was in the bathroom but held back, fearing she might overhear. All he'd volunteer on his own were a few generalities. "I'll be glad, right glad, when this is over," he said. "Back to the usual—speeders, DUI's, stray cattle, a rape maybe or a wife-beating, a little Saturday night brawling . . . Normal life."

Thirteen

What the Black Box Said

IT'S ME AGAIN—Francie.

I never did catch up with that old man who'd been snagged on the fence wire, the one who asked me if I was from Lübeck. He must have wandered around for quite a while, finally coming to rest at the Dairy Queen half the way between here and Hardesty. He'd caused a stir at the DQ, trying to order "crept locks" or some such, repeating himself, growing louder and angrier each time the girl at the counter said, "Please?" Then she'd hailed the manager. The manager had never heard of any such dish either, but he'd noticed the shape of the man's tie and the fact that he wasn't wearing any shoes—those things tipped him off. He slipped the counter girl a note about what number to call, and somehow sweet-talked the old man into sitting down with him over a cup of hot chocolate.

The sheriff had arrived shortly, with the old man's daughter in tow. It had been a strange reunion, to hear tell: she'd hugged him and wept; he'd stared at her and inquired what sort of business she was in. And so—so to speak—they'd connected.

That old man had been my only real link with the crash. I hadn't gone out to the Wooten place to hunt for souvenirs or spilt money. Most of the people I worked with had at least tried to. I wasn't even curious to take a gawk at the field. Only one crash in anybody's life, I figure; I'd had mine when my folks were killed. It was hit-and-run; for hours, nobody noticed—a drunken teenager plowing into them with his pickup, flinging them out onto the blacktop like things thrown away, and racing on.

Today's Sunday. A day I never liked, and here I was with a cold on top of it, and it was raining on top of that —so misery upon misery. Couple of late nights filling in at the Lounge, plus all the wild weather we'd been having lately—going from winter to spring to winter again in the space of hours—must've done me in.

Normally I'd be playing the piano at Senior Citizens from noon to three. It's a pretty beat-up instrument, but surprisingly well tuned, well enough for what's needed, and I'm free to rove the keyboard while the seniors are busy eating, before the supervised singing begins. I don't really object to going there—I earn something, and it gives a little shape to the long day. I take the opportunity to improvise while they're sitting at the long tables, stuffing their faces with food and talk, not paying the least attention to me. When I run out of ideas and need coasting time, I'll summon up the old standbys, the primer stuff, "Für Elise" and "Chopsticks," so I'm never really at a loss. After the meal comes the singalong. They'll be sitting in classroom rows around the piano, raising their hands for their favorites, "How Great Thou Art," and "One Day at a Time"—*my* least favorite, it's so plodding. And, nearly always, they'll want "Listen to the Mockingbird." Jim Titus joins in with his fiddle on that one, playing it close to the bridge, trilling on the bird chorus, and taking lo-ong glides up and down the fingerboard, ending on a double stop each round. Pretty fancy fiddling for an old man and hard to forget. The sound is piercing, in the highest register.

And, every so often, Maggie Campbell will rise up with her walker and start strutting in time to the music, with Jim Titus swaying and high-stepping alongside, so we've got us a dance. Then, chances are, there's a birthday, and we do the traditional for it. It's when they start up with the likes of "I Wonder Who's Kissing Her Now" and I gaze out over those ranks of gray heads that I begin to wonder: *Is this for real? Have you flipped your lid, Francie, or what?* But it is real, so help me, and they tend to lead here, with the piano only following along: "I wonder who's kissing her now . . . I wonder who's teaching her how . . ." It always amazes me, the way their frail voices swell up on that one.

But I wouldn't be playing there today, not with this cold, or low-grade flu, or whatever. Too much effort and I might be contagious. Besides, I'd be slurry and miss notes —I was all doped up.

Like I say, Sundays tend to be pretty slow for me— church being the only show in town. So I have to admit I missed the Senior Citizens just a little bit. Just a twinge. I was curious to know what they'd be wanting to sing this particular Sunday, and whether they'd be talking up the crash or politely sidestepping the subject. A dreary day, the rain wasn't stopping, and I thought of all the preachers going at it right this very minute. Plenty of opportunity in the crash—for them. Plenty of *fodder* there. Brother Pipes came to mind. Only a minute or two late if I wanted to tune into him. I was kind of wondering . . . Not that I ever expected to be surprised by anything Brother Pipes chose to say: he'd been around too long. Still—I'd be interested to hear his account of the crash. I'd been told he was out of town when it happened—he'd missed it by a day and a night.

He'd already started—but one thing about Brother Pipes, you can pick him up anytime, anywhere, and land at the same place, exactly where he means for you to be. Impossible to get lost—in the hearing of it, at least. He didn't sound too far into the message part, still moping along at cruising speed, and nowhere near weeping yet. Fast, loud, gnashing and weeping's how he usually winds up.

"You ask me, Brother Pipes, will we ever get back to

normal in Bounds? Will we ever be the same as we use to be? Brothers and sisters, I pray not! Not the same old mountain of satisfactions! Not the same old careless life! No more business as usual. Not after this! God's pointing a finger. One day you're not going to see the sun come up. Flight 582 was God's pointing, the fiery furnace, the place of testing, the sevenfold heat, the writing on the wall, the hand of God writing on the wall! It's coming to you—by cancer, by blood pressure, by falling out of the sky. Doesn't matter who you are—the hand of God is writing on the wall. Read it and weep—*mene, mene, tekel*— ME-NE—God hath numbered thy kingdom and finished it. *TE-KEL*—thou art weighed in the balance and found wanting. The hand has written, watch the hand!"

Another thing about Brother Pipes is—you may not like him or agree with him, but he sure does get your attention. Like two people combing your hair at the same instant! Maybe it was my cold, this nasty head cold, that made him especially chilling. In the pauses, I could hear the rain ticking on the glass. It was a slow soft rain . . . made me sleepy to listen to. Truth to tell, I'd been in sort of a doze ever since the crash, ever since that dream . . . Caught out between two worlds maybe. Between the voice of Brother Pipes and the rain . . . it was like drowsing off and being yanked awake, drowsing off and . . .

"Stricken by your love, Father—"

That roused me. I reached over and turned the volume down. I never watch television preaching—none of the preachers in Bounds had gotten on television yet—though I thought Brother Pipes would be the first to, if ever that came to pass. Him and that church he built! People pass-

ing on the road always gawking at it. That's exactly what
he planned on. It's *different,* that I'll grant. Suppose to
look like a covered wagon—one of those hooped ceilings,
flared at the front end. Always looked like a great big
bullhorn to me. A bullhorn pointed at the ear of God.

And that was something Brother Pipes wouldn't ever
have any need of, in my opinion, with that big voice of
his, full of almighty soundings and resoundings. All those
"whosoevers" and "the Lord saiths"! I never trusted him
for a minute—the way he claps your hand in two of his,
like a man that wants your vote. That extra pressure of
the palm, inclining his head and winking with smiles:
"How about it, Francie? How about singing in *my* choir?"

He's got all the answers to all the questions you'll ever
ask and then some for the questions you'd never think to
ask. It's all one big ball of yarn, unraveling as foretold.
Creation and Fall, the Ark and the Tower, the Law and
the overcoming of the Law, the crash of Flight 582
wrapped in there, somewhere in between the Resurrection
and the Rapture of the saved. The Tribulation of the Earth
would come after the Rapture, and the White Throne
Judgment after the Rapture. As it was written in the beginning of time, and unfolding as foretold.

"Look up! Look up for the biggest trend!"

I knew in advance how it would go from here—the
trump, the scrolls, the vials poured out—I'd only get furious, so why bother to listen? Yes, but I didn't know all the
details. I was curious to know if he'd mention Glenna
Wooten's field—just whatever sense he made of that. I
guess none of us had really gotten over the plane's coming
down in Bounds.

"You say, Preacher, you're too hard! No, I'm not. You just think on this: seven crew members, ninety-two souls on board—on a pleasure cruise, many of them. There was a lottery winner on board, you know that? She won big—over a million dollars. I won't tell you her name or the name of the state she won it in, it doesn't matter. Let me mention only that she was traveling first class. She won—she lost. First class to where? You think a minute on that—

"So there they were, going along, on a pleasure cruise, the lottery winner going first class. Think of all that pleasure! Imagine—forty-three dead, our lottery winner among them. Twenty-seven injured, many of them critically. Twenty-nine saved. Call that pleasure? Some pleasure! Consider the hell over which you hang. You say, Preacher, who you talking about? I'm talking about you, brother. I'm talking about you, sister. I'm talking about first and last things. And I'm talking about God—

"God is alive and Jesus is the only begotten son of God. He is God. Without question. Without comment. Turn to Him—turn to Him!

"Think about it—while you've still got a minute to think. Did you ever wonder—what were they thinking, what were they talking about, what were they hoping, those passengers on Flight 582? What were they thinking about when the plane went down? *Playboy* magazine? Their cash flow? Their pretty things? Think so? Well, I'm here to tell you there wasn't time for any of that. Their watches stopped. On the instant. Know what time it was? I'll tell you. Their watches stopped on that instant: it was two-sixteen post meridiem—it was too late—it was call-on-the-Lord-in-vain time. The skies were as granite.

"No time to change! No time to compromise! We better live every day like that. We better live every single hour of every single day like that! But, no, we've got our own pews and we're gonna sit in them and not get up. We're fat, increased with goods, satisfied and needing nothing—Laodicea, lukewarm, and ready for the big heat. Well, Flight 582 is the big heat, the writing on the wall. *The moving finger writes and having writ . . .*"

The rain hushed, then gusted up, then hushed again, as if it, too, was listening. Brother Pipes was on to explaining what the black box was, how it wasn't really black but bright red or orange or yellow, and how the cockpit voice recorder was stowed inside it to tell the tale after the plane went down.

"Know what the black box says? It says, 'Whoop! . . . Whoop! . . . Pull up! Pull up!' That's a recorded voice, the last warning voice before the pilot shouts, 'Position doubtful!' or 'Mayday!' or 'Sinking . . .' Five times out of six, the last words, the last words of the pilot before the roaring begins, before the sounds of impact deafens all, are curses. Four-letter curses! Time and again!

"Know what the black box said—the one they found in Bounds? 'We've lost it!' Brothers and sisters, we've lost it! Fall on your knees—we've lost it—" His voice swelled, boomed out, crowded the kitchen.

"God makes His power known—"

And that was it. Brother Pipes had gone on for too long. His theme song, "Are You Washed in the Blood?" covered his voice. Must have been pre-recorded. I knew Brother

Pipes had been cut off because I'd heard him enough times to catch on to the rhythm of his service. He'd been only warming up for the end. There was the altar call yet to come, then the special hymn of invitation for the day, then his closing "Amen and Amen and Amen again!"—pounding in the tent stakes, as he liked to say.

I stood up and stretched in the pause that followed. Peeked out the window: the rain was coming down faster now, blistering the glass. When the opening announcement of Skyview Apostolic Assembly came on, without music, offering "the sincere meat of God's word," I reached over and clicked the radio off. I'd had my dose of religion for the day. After brimstone—sincere meat! Is it any wonder I can't stomach it?

Fourteen

Stories

WE WERE MOVING ALONG nicely. At least, the mayor was. My last interview in a long go-round, and it was all I could do to keep from nodding. Too much high-density time. I was avoiding coffee by then, trying to keep my hands from shaking. One more cup, I thought, and they'd have to dry me out on a detox ward. I was still functioning, though, checking over old facts and stumbling on a few new ones. Try as I might, my notes tended to slope steeply downwards—looked like the words were about to slide off the page—but my handwriting was remarkably legible under the circumstances. Not much new, so far. I wrote: *John Bounds surveyed site 1885—incorp. 1893.* The mayor smiled. "October seventeenth is the centennial. Try and come round for it. Enjoy yourself and give us a little ink. We could use some *good* publicity—after this—" He made a creaking quarter turn in his swivel chair. "Let me make sure I got this straight—you're from the Fort Worth, not the Dallas, paper, that right?"

"Right," I said. "You're not from these parts?" he added. "Right again," I said, tapping my pen, hoping to signal my disinclination to go on with this particular subject.

He took the hint, shifted tracks, and soon was droning on like a chamber of commerce brochure. "Count seed— you count the future," he declared, quoting somebody or other. "We grow wheat, haygrazer, milo, triticale . . ." I asked him to spell it, that last one; he did, and I wrote after it: *hybrid—rye and ??* Just trying to stay alert—it wasn't a detail I ever planned on using.

"Soybeans, native grasses for forage . . ." The mayor was on a roll. "Bet you never saw grass growing in drill rows like any other cash crop!" I hadn't—or hadn't known I had. He went on to praise the climate—"two-hundred-five days between killing frosts"—the work ethic —"nobody keeps bankers hours in Bounds." No unions, so no feather-bedding, deals done with a handshake, low crime rate, churchgoing folks by and large, no pollution yet—I'd heard this sort of recital before. Couple of fifty-acre industrial sites, waiting for the right customers to come along. "You might give us a plug on that." Utility rates hard to beat, and there'd be some tax abatement as a sweetener. It was all more or less standard, the mayor's line, but then, abruptly, he'd about-faced. Clamped shut. Leaned well forward, over the tiny Texas flag on his pen-stand. The silence—it was pretty disconcerting.

"So," I said, "where were we?"

"Tell me again exactly what you're after—" he said.

"A little background," I reminded him. "Anything you think we ought to know about Bounds. Anything you want to tell the world—here's your chance."

Maybe I was too direct. "Some chance!" he said. "Some opportunity!" Then he seemed to recollect himself. Back to the theme of what a nice town it was. "We've got a prayer chain going," he wanted me to know. "For the victims and their families. That oughta tell you something about us. We won't be selling T-shirts to advertise the crash, unlike some other towns I could name. They'd be cashing in on all the publicity—T-shirts, bumper stickers, buttons for the tourists. You know, you've seen those things, how they print them right up. We're not like that."

He ran on a bit then about a single exception that proved the rule—a woman in Bounds, name of Judy Miller, who claimed she'd foretold the accident. She'd written a prediction on a scrap of paper—something about a misfortune coming in the spring—and baked it into her annual fortune cake at the county fair. That was way back in September. This Miller lady, it seemed, planned on writing a magazine article about the crash and how she forecast it. But she was the only one thinking of cashing in.

"Right now," he said, "with all the television people

and emergency crews here and everything, there's a run on
goods and services. We don't object to that—I'd be lying if
I said otherwise—but there's also litter, noise, congestion
—those things we can live without. Another week or two,
all you temporary people will be gone and things will start
getting back to normal. We like the company—not the
occasion for it. We like the attention—not all of it—but a
certain amount of it from time to time. I expect we'll feel
slow for a little bit, but—"

And then he blew the interview. Just exploded. I don't
know what sparked it. I might have been looking momen-
tarily cross-eyed at him; I'd been trying to bite back a
yawn. He pitched forward, stabbing the air with his fore-
finger, aiming straight for my heart. Talking fast:

"Don't think for one minute that people in Bounds
don't know where we stand with you people coming in
from the city. We're the old folks, still back on the farm—
we're—how do you put it?—*quaint,* salt of the earth and
don't know where you'd ever be without us, but you're
always much too busy with your important lives to give us
the time of day. Unless something like this happens. Or
you want to dump something toxic on us! Don't think we
don't know. Any day now we could dry up and blow
away without anybody down in Austin or Dallas or Hous-
ton ever turning a hair or even noticing we're gone. Not
that there aren't compensations for that, compensations
aplenty—peace and quiet and old-time values—but I want
you to know that *we* know where we stand.

"You just tell them about how many people in Bounds
have offered to give blood and help out with food and
blankets and transportation and such. Just whatever ways

we could. That's the kind of town we are: we pull together. Got to—to survive. You tell them that.

"We may be small and off the main road, but we're a
nice town. Soon as we recover from this and everybody
outside forgets about us, we'll be nicer yet. We'll be just
fine. Come by and see."

I'd touched a nerve, all right.

After the interview, I was still too keyed up to sleep.
What I needed was to slow down gradually, so I turned in
at the first place. The sign said *Nick of Time Lounge*,
something like that. Or *Tick of Time,* maybe. Whatever . . .

I took a booth to myself, hoping to unwind over a couple of Buds. The place was only half full, but couldn't
have been noisier. I recognized one of the grips, a camera-
man, and a few of the technical people from a Dallas television crew. And some of the locals looked vaguely familiar.

The waitress was a hefty dishwater blonde. Corn fed
and freckled—peasant legs. Strictly local variety. She wore
a nametag, but I was so cockeyed, even before I'd started
on beer, that I misread it as "Raunchie," sounding like
"raunchy." "Are you?" I winked, pointing to the badge,
making a dumb joke of it. "That's Francie," she said icily,
"for Frances. You ready to order yet?" No smile, no non-
sense, not one word to spare beyond "You want chips
with that?"—the bare functional minimum. Don't know
why I was so stressed by her: she was the type of woman I
wouldn't ordinarily have touched with a ten-foot pole. No
ring on her finger and no wonder. She set the bill down
beside me soon as she brought the beer. It was neatly

totaled, tax included: she'd finished with me. Never bothered to look my way again. So I knew I'd triggered a nerve, same as with the mayor. Foot in my mouth, or face in my foot—I'd kicked myself.

It seemed to be growing noisier by the minute. Words crackling in the air all around me. I remember a woman saying, "It doesn't make sense," and a man answering, "What does? Shit happens—every day." What I couldn't get out of my mind was this image—a thing that hadn't really registered at the time—a kid's toothbrush, pale blue, laying out in the field. I thought of how strange it was, how I never actually cry. Just get a prickling, this crawling sensation, in my scalp. My scalp weeps, maybe . . . why I'm half bald. That was the level of my thinking right then.

I was whipped, wasted, my tiredness as hard to ignore as thumbs on the eyeballs. The beer wasn't helping. When I walked out onto the parking lot, I tripped on the speed bump and was thrown to my knees. Nothing broken or torn, but I was shaken by it. I reminded myself to drive very slowly. Best to creep along in second all the way.

For miles up the road, the motels were taken. I was pretty close to the Hardesty town limits before I found one with a vacancy. I recall swinging into a numbered parking space and cutting my headlights—then blotto. Threw myself on the bed without trying to undress, and slept for ten hours solid, waking only once to stagger to the bathroom and take a leak, an all-time record for me. Before eight, I got up for good—not nearly enough shut-eye but a substantial first installment. I'd have to catch up gradually.

I had the television going in the bedroom while I shaved. And fretted over the hair I'd lost in the past few days! The program was onto weather. All I could make out was that "friendly skies" were coming back, not how long they'd stay. Another strange thing, I thought, staring at myself through a half mask of lather: how quickly you slip back into the humdrum normal. I'd seen people with whole swatches of skin peeled off, and here I was worrying about millimeters of scalp exposed. Could you beat that? But I knew it was only a distraction. In an hour or two, I'd be back on the scene.

Mostly, I love my job. There'd be no point in putting up with what I have to put up with if I didn't. The pay is pitiful, considering all the hours I put in, the daily wear and tear of getting places and getting there fast—a deadline every minute. Not to mention the stress of editors like Mo Burns—"there's a number, an exact number"—breathing down your neck. Mo has a motto from Harry Truman framed on his desk: I DON'T GIVE THEM HELL. I JUST TELL THEM THE TRUTH AND THEY THINK IT'S HELL. Isn't easy, working for a man with a motto like that.

Still . . . there are compensations. Curiosity has always been a passion with me. Reporting gives me a license to ask questions, and to meet up with all kinds of people I wouldn't otherwise. And, good grief, I even love the smell of newsprint, the way it dirties your fingers—the smear of big ink news.

When I was a cub starting out, what I liked best about my job was the endless variety of it, my sense of boundless expectation, starting over each day afresh. But lately, before the crash, it seemed like the chances of something new turning up were definitely diminishing. Maybe there weren't so many stories, after all. I thought of that priest, making the same gestures over everyone, motions bounded by some ancient template handed down. For him, I thought, there's only one story in the world: *born, suffered, died.* With an epilogue for the faithful: *raised and redeemed.* Or, for those of doubtful faith: *the story made whole.* But, as for me, I still believed the world was full of stories—maybe not an endless supply, but plenty of really different ones, most of them destined to remain incomplete.

I never did grasp what the priest was up to that first night, but by the time I got to him, just before sunup, he looked as exhausted as I felt, and I cautioned myself: *don't press.* I still couldn't figure it. Anybody ever do anything without motive? Not that I've noticed. I have to admit that my first thought when I saw him dabbing them all with oil and blessing them, making the sign of the cross over them, was: he's making them all Catholic. I'm still not convinced that wasn't what he was up to.

Me—I'm Presbyterian—Sunday school for a couple years, on my mother's side, and nothing on my father's side. That makes me—what? Guess I'd have to say: nothing, really. And I guard that nothing pretty zealously. So the priest made me nervous. What did he know that I didn't? Anything? Where was God when the lights went out? I'd like an answer. People always say that seeing something like this crash makes a believer out of you, but a believer, I ask, in what? In the god of cycles, maybe, the god of ruins. No expectation but to be crushed, sooner or later. Only other sense I could make of it was that maybe all the gods who'd ever been thought of were true and were slugging it out with one another—the barking gods, the bleating gods, you name it.

I'd been thinking I might do a follow-up with the priest later the next day. Start all over from scratch when we were both wide-awake, but, as it turned out, it was one thing after another from the first night on—I never did manage to get back to him. The cold took over soon as the fire died away, and I had to keep moving, if only to keep my blood circulating. It was cold, cave cold, the fillings in my teeth ringing with the chill.

Somewhere along in that first shift, I'd snatched a few hours of sleep in the back of my car—enough to give me a second wind. Then I worked two days straight, plus the night in-between, before my replacement, Matty Langer, arrived. Matty's our farm and ranch reporter; he'd been wanting a change of pace, and here it was. He'd brought along fresh clothes, too—his own. I was touched by it. Matty's a little heavier than me, but not that much—his old togs would do. I'd given him a quick rundown on what to look out for, told him I'd cover the mayor before turning in, then hit the ground running, like the first of those survivors.

Simply luxurious . . . the feel of fresh clothes after a shower. My only change in the past few days had been into the work clothes I kept in the trunk of the car. Everything I'd worn was stiff with filth, giving off a thick musk of fuel and scorched earth; sweat and body odor were the least of it. I doubted they'd ever wash out, and ended up chucking the whole mess, shirt to socks, into the giant dumpster out back of the motel.

After breakfast and a call to my chief, I'd be taking over again. Along about nine, give or take five, I should be back in the field, ready to wind things up. Before that, I made it my business to scout out as many newspapers as I could. I spread them out on the bed and dove in.

The big story in *USA Today* was a feature interview with three passengers who'd walked away from the crash unscathed. They were using some of my quotes—without attribution. I'd scooped the story and others were building on it. It irked me, but that's the name of the game. You have to keep moving just to stay alive in my business. I don't stew about it overmuch, at least, not like I used to. And, anyway, the copy desk would be cutting me down to a couple of paragraphs in a few days. Then it would be on to the next thing—and the next.

The Fort Worth paper had a front-page feature on natives of the metroplex who'd been passengers on the flight. The paper was still printing passenger lists—names of those hospitalized and in what condition, names of those treated and let go, names of the deceased. By now, "missing" or "not accounted for" meant: presumed dead. The process of identifying remains would never be chronicled —too grisly. I located Matty's account of the mop-up in Bounds. It wasn't bad. Alongside it was a national news feature on mixups in the fatality count. I'd contributed to that, but A.P. had claimed the full account, crediting it to their own man. So, anyway. The byline read: Ross Turner. Did I know him? This bit was new: seems it wasn't only the toddlers riding their mothers' laps and not being listed in the flight manifest that caused an error in the count, there was some suspicion of a stowaway as well. Another

thing, in a box, four inches of print—an appetizer, really
—offering some informed guesses as to damage settle-
ments. In the weeks and months to come, this story would
move to first place.

There was a neat little item in the Dallas paper on flight
and terminal operations at DFW, including the resump-
tion of the normal run for Maxim Flight 582, San Diego
to New York, now back on schedule. And a backgrounder, kind of late in my view, on the aircraft itself.
Vital statistics: crew, payload, horsepower, fuel capacity,
maximum speed, cruising speed, cruising altitude. Hard to
believe they hadn't covered most of this before, yet everybody assumes that Fort Worth is the poor stepsister of
Dallas. There was a mention of the number of flights our
particular plane had accomplished before the crash.
Again, that was something we'd covered early on.

The best story of all about Flight 582 hadn't surfaced in
print. Chances were, it never would. I'd done my
damndest to track it down and would do more if I could,
but there were only two witnesses able to give testimony,
and one of them really wasn't a witness—she'd heard the
other, the only real witness talking about it. So I had one
direct testimony and one hearsay report, not enough to go
on. It had all happened in "a split second." Exactly how
long is a split second? I suppose what he meant was: not
enough time to think or take responsibility. The witness—
I'll call him Joe Blow—had been the last person out the
emergency exit before flashover occurred. Everyone standing behind him was trapped in the flames and perished,
and he, Joe Blow, knew he should have perished along
with them. He'd been pushing forward—they all had—

and he'd nearly knocked over the gentleman in front of him. The passengers had formed what he called "a line." From what others said, it must have been more like a free-for-all with everybody bunching up at the exits, Joe Blow trampling along with everybody else. He'd shoved the gent in front of him who'd turned aside, then saying, "Oh, excuse me," and given up his place to Blow. The old man had spoken as casually as if he'd been keeping a seat or a coat for someone, only holding on to it until the owner showed up and then, why naturally . . . Joe Blow never did get a good look at the man whose place he'd taken. The cabin was thick with smoke. He—Blow—had an impression that the gentleman was old, his hair whitish, but he wasn't sure. Maybe it was easier to think of him as being old. Beyond that, all Joe Blow could remember was that the man had been wearing some sort of muffler or scarf. But there was so much confusion in that "split second" before flashover, he couldn't even be sure of the scarf. Joe Blow, the man who escaped, was haunted by the man who stayed behind, a man whose name he didn't know.

That was one story I'd love to have snared. I doubted I ever would, though. A sentimental tale, old-fashioned. Not a bit fresh. For all I know, there might be a tale like this for every crash. I didn't know if it was true or not, but it might have been—it ought to have been. I wanted for it to be true.

THREE

Fifteen

Visitors

IN THE LAND OF THE LIVING, we tried to move on. The smell of burning lingered over Bounds for much of the first week after the crash. School was called off that first Tuesday so that mothers could be with their children and offer what comfort and understanding they could. Janet Callahan came to me in tears after morning Mass, wanting to know what to do about Susie. Only five, she'd seemed to take in nothing when her older brothers talked up the crash in vivid and gory detail but, not long after, she started throwing her Cabbage Patch doll out the window and laughing as it fell. This was the same precious doll she'd waited for all summer and fall and had finally come to her with toy adoption papers at Christmas.

Susie wasn't the only problem. Don Bateson mentioned in passing that he'd taken his son Arthur over to a doctor in Hardesty, who said the boy needed tranquilizers and prescribed a low dose of barbiturates for him. Arthur, who's a bright, outgoing eleven-year-old, the last child you'd expect to be causing trouble, had to be practically dragged out to the car these days. Not only that—he'd refused to board the school bus, and resisted leaving the house for any reason. When Don finally forced him to go to the doctor, the boy started crying and wouldn't stop until his father promised to drive very slowly. They had to creep along. Each time Dan moved a sliver over thirty, the boy would break into hysterical weeping.

Actually, we're *all* jumpy. Only the other day, as I was taking my usual walk, a feather fell out of the air and brushed my forehead. I jolted back as though I'd been stabbed. Only a feather!

For two weeks, I couldn't preach on the crash at all. We had a rosary on the evening of the first day, and the church was full to bursting. On the days following, I leaned heavily on the lectionary and the prescribed Lenten readings. I did offer intercessions for the victims—asking that mercy, pity, peace, and love dwell with them and with their families. This called for no real thought on my part. I invited prayers of petition from the congregation. There was a groundswell of response. Left to myself, though, I could not pray over what I'd seen. I spoke to my tape recorder about the crash—a sort of "debriefing"—but I wouldn't, by any stretch of the word, have called this praying. I listened to my parishioners and to the visitors who stopped by. Listened and consoled with whatever was needful. I didn't attempt to fathom—I had no idea—what God was up to. Quite a few folks in Bounds had no doubt whatsoever that the crash of Flight 582 had been a judgment of some kind. I'd picked up Brother Pipes on the radio a couple of times; he was getting considerable mileage from the disaster. For him, it was clearly "the hand of God at work," "God speaking in power." I was not at all convinced of this. On the cross over the altar at Blessed Redeemer was another God—the stricken God whom I professed to follow. He'd spoken seven words of lament, and then no words at all—how then could I presume to speak? The possible existence of some master equation able to account for the havoc I'd seen was chilling to me—I've never, in my heart of hearts, prayed to the God of gravitation, the God of the melting of metals. Not even to the moral bookkeeping God, the God of the balancing of ledgers. So I avoided telling people what God was up to—I had my hands full explaining what *we* were up to, what I was up to, with this devastation in our midst.

Naturally, I talked it over with my confessor. His advice was sensible: he warned me in no uncertain terms of the likelihood of burnout, and urged me to take time off. I agreed to let things sift, but I couldn't take time off. Not now. Leaving struck me as unthinkable now. I had work to do, even if it wasn't clear from day to day what it would be, or how I would manage it. I was mostly in the dark.

In the newspaper photographs taken that first night, I am and am not there. My face never comes into definition. It's as though I'm wearing a mask. In one photo, I'm only a silhouette, could be a knobbed and leaning tree, backlit by fire. In another, just this: three elements: stole, hand, and forehead. Mine is the stole and the hand extended. *In persona Christi*—that part seems right, that's what we were taught—acting not in ourselves, but *through* Christ. And, it's strange . . . it's almost as if the camera picks this up. In more ways than one, I am mostly in the dark.

One of the F.A.A. investigators, a new one, stopped by yesterday to go over, for a second time, what I'd seen at the crash site. I wish I could have been more helpful. He recorded our conversation, and interrupted on points of fine detail whenever I seemed careless or too casual in my choice of words. He had some charts, sketches of planes, slanted in different angles of descent. I was supposed to pick out the angle that best matched the descent of Flight 582. I had to remind him that I hadn't actually witnessed the plane going down, only the stall beforehand. When I'd told him all I could remember, I tried to turn the tables on him and find out what they'd been able to piece together so far.

He wasn't permitted to reveal that, and could only speak in the most general terms. There might not be a verdict for months, or years, to come. And, even then, the most they could ever presume to uncover was "the probable cause, or causes"—they'd never be absolutely sure.

"It's quite different from the kind of certainties you

must be used to," he said, and I didn't bother to contradict him.

What I gathered from his extremely guarded account was that all the obvious signs pointed to the weather, extreme turbulence, and possible wind shear. That deaths by flailing were evidence for this. On the other hand, the shreddings from limb to limb and certain bendings of the metal suggested possible disintegration within the plane—an explosion or structural defect. There were no signs pointing to sabotage, but much remained to be sorted through. Injuries were being cataloged and coordinated with seating arrangements.

I also gathered—from someone else, a conversation overheard in the field—that the tailpiece was somehow suspect. The man spoke of "a sting in the tail." It *was* curious—that particular section being so wholly intact, shaped so perfectly like the letter "T". And it *was* a little scorpion-like, once they'd mentioned it, such is the power of suggestion. For some reason, the tail assembly was the last of the big pieces of wreckage to be cleared from the field.

I was relieved that my duties in Bounds excused me from having to speak at the big memorial service for the next of kin. That was held in Dallas at a church near the airport. Far better that somebody else speak, someone who hadn't actually been at the scene of the crash. Lately, I've had very short nerves for proclamative clatter. I knew they'd be intoning from First Corinthians somewhere along the line—"glory" and "imperishability" sure to be worked into it. Given the images that haunted me, words like those would have made me cough.

But I wasn't excused from the follow-up. Since I'd been present at the last moments of many of the deceased, their relatives kept stopping in at Blessed Redeemer, seeking a word with me. "Stopping in" makes it sound more casual than it was. Turns out, the airline, the carrier company, had provided the transportation in nearly every case. Most of the relatives stayed over in Bounds for at least one night.

I kept the church open night and day, and I'd stumble in, only half-awake for my early Mass, to find the sanctuary full to cloying with the too-sweet smell of hothouse flowers. The steps leading to the altar would be heaped with roses, carnations, and lilies. Sometimes, framed photographs appeared among the flowers. Happy faces mostly, smiling out of an earlier time. When the photographs failed to disappear, I decided we were meant to keep them, so I put up a table in the vestibule and placed them on it. I added a visitors' sign-in book, which filled up rapidly in the weeks and months to come.

Not everyone seeks me out. But those who do always ask to visit the field—"to see the place." What they really want, I guess, is to share in those last moments of flight. Glenna Wooten gave me permission to bring people out. "Won't be growing anything on that field for a long while," she told me. "What good is it to me now? Any use it might have, any comfort it might give them to have a look, I'd be glad for."

Usually the sun is shining when we get there. The field looks barren and scarred, with only a trace of the original furrowing at the edges. Yet, here and there, small patches of mud are already greening up. Our skies, these days, tend to be bright and cloudless, purged of all evil humors. We could still see chunks of the wreckage at first, then less and less as the days wore on. The crash investigators were reconstructing the plane, connecting the fragments and webbing the empty spaces with chicken wire, was what I'd heard. But that was going on in one of the hangars at the old Love Field Airport in Dallas. Only a few members of the F.A.A. team remained on site after the first week, one of them staring at the ground and taking notes, and one moving, slowly clockwise, round the field, trailing a leafbag over his shoulder and stooping, from time to time, to retrieve a shard of something too small to see from where I stood.

"So this is where it was. This was the last thing he saw . . . *If* he was conscious . . . was he?" All of the relatives say pretty much the same thing.

"It looks so peaceful."

"Yes," I say, remembering.

It doesn't matter where they come from—Bangkok or Tucson, wherever—the heart's in the same pocket. They all cling to the same hopes. A Japanese father wanted to find the exact spot where his son died. If the boy had fallen from the roof, he argued, there'd be a mark in the pavement. He had to find that spot to be able to pray properly, to be able to say that he'd laid his son's spirit to rest. This was the only sense I could make of his long outpouring, phrasebook English garbled with tears.

It was, of course, impossible to stand on that spot even if, conceivably, we could have found it. The field itself was still off limits to everyone except the investigators. So I stood, and he knelt at the fence line. Not wanting to embarrass him, I left him to it, withdrawing a few yards off. Then I began to feel awkward simply standing there. I might have gone back and knelt alongside him but, by then, it seemed too late, an afterthought. I'd missed the natural, the graceful, thing, and anything after that would have been clumsy. And, to tell the truth, whatever it was that had first prevented me still dragged at my feet.

Later, he asked me to go back to the field with him; he wanted to place a funeral wreath on the fence. Other wreaths soon followed. When one of them, a ramshackle bunch of silk roses and paper leaves, seemed ready to fall and scatter, I noticed Glenna Wooten out there, securing it with wire.

So many questions, so many hurts . . . "We waited for hours and they told us nothing. Just kept changing the arrival time. Then they removed the flight listing from the board. All along they *knew* and told us nothing." This became a familiar story.

Catholic visitors would come and sit in the back pews during Mass. During an unscheduled hour, I'd often find them in the forward pews, praying silently or saying the rosary. They were clearly more at home on the church premises, but I couldn't say they seemed less troubled than the others. One of the Catholics, a young man from Tucson, left a note in the visitors' book indicating that his father had perished in the crash, but he never dropped into the office or tried to get in touch with me. He showed up at our main Sunday Mass. He genuflected and made the sign of the cross in all the right places, but he didn't come up for Communion. Didn't open his mouth once that I noticed, not for the profession of faith, not even for the great Amen. I learned later that he'd placed a fifty-dollar bill in the collection plate, but he'd wadded it up so tightly it was about the size of a pill. An offering, and a generous one, to be sure, to a church like ours, but mixed with so much anger that the creases would not come out.

A surprising number of the people who stopped by to visit with me were Asians of one kind or another. We communicated, with many fumblings, over the divides of language and creed. One of the later visitors—a certain Mr. Adab from Karachi, whose first name I didn't catch—was quite Westernized. His English was impeccable, though a bit formal; it was all "to be sure" and "*ve*-ry" and "bloody well" and "quite!" His dress matched his diction, startling for here—pin-striped suit, snowy white shirt with double cuffs and cuff-links, and what I assumed was a school tie. He was "England-educated. Oxford—not one of those red-brick rugby colleges." He wanted me to know this. It struck me as an odd occasion to insist upon such distinctions, though I tried to seem properly impressed.

I'd noticed a certain coolness and composure in him from the first and, sure enough, he turned out to be a somewhat distant cousin of the deceased. Since he had business in the States, he'd been delegated by the family to visit the site. He spoke calmly of "destiny" and "fate." I drove him over to the field where he added his wreath to the others. By now, there was a long string of wreaths ranged along the wire. He said what they always say: "How peaceful . . ."

It was. And in the following days, it continued to be nearly always peaceful. The afternoon I took Mr. Adab out to the field was one of those lustrous blue days. A mild breeze welling up every now and then, a sort of brimming. I want to say *brimming and blessing,* that was the feeling. The struggles of winter seemed long over. It was an illusion, of course, only a reprieve, but we basked in it, standing there. The blackened topsoil had been carted off; the exposed earth was iodine-colored, freshly dozed, and the green was poking up. Weeds, I suspected, pepperweed and the first shoots of Johnsongrass, but even weeds were welcome now.

Back in my office, the conversation became pointed. "Did you bless him?" he came at me abruptly, then softened, "if I may ask . . ."

"I blessed and anointed each and every one."

He was silent for a moment and seemed to be studying the clock on the wall. I couldn't read his face, only the inquisitorial jut of his head. He had his back to the light; the window behind him was flooded with brightness. "So," he resumed, "that is good," sounding not at all convinced of it. "And did he—*could* he—tell you about himself?"

I couldn't recall that. "There were many," I reminded him. "Some—a few—were semiconscious. Most were beyond all telling. He was a Moslem and died a Moslem, if that's what bothers you."

He sighed and said softly, "Aacha," something like that, like a soft sneeze. "So you blessed him in—how should I say—some sort of Esperanto?"

"Wrong," I said emphatically. "I blessed him in the language I know. I trust the translation will be taken care of."

Mr. Adab sighed. "I once thought pluralism might be possible," he said. "I thought of Lebanon as a model. And now look at Beirut! Hell on earth, wouldn't you say?"

"From what I've heard," I said, "but there are other factors—"

"Let us agree not to disguise our differences."

"By all means," I agreed. "Whatever's on your mind."

He went on a bit, predictably, I thought, about Christian intolerance—the Crusades, the Inquisition; I recited my *mea culpas,* said we'd come along since then. I mentioned that I hadn't seen all that much in the way of tolerance from the Islamic regimes lately. He shifted back to the deceased. He recalled the young man's charitableness, his mildness of temper.

I knew that wasn't the end of it, but I didn't anticipate the discussion that followed. It was no part of my training; he was the first Moslem I'd talked to, *ever.* He started briefing me on Islam, assuring me of his love for Mary—Mariam, he called her. He reminded me that Abraham was his father in faith, too. That done, he launched directly into his difficulties with the Trinity. His argument was hedged with politeness, prefaced "with all respect" and "if I may be frank," but sharp, plenty sharp. Why turn qualities into entities—into persons? That was the gist of it. And that was only the beginning. His main difficulty with the Christian faith he put down to "temperamental differences."

"Oh?" I was curious to hear more.

"It is a very beautiful religion, the Christian. Beautiful, but so very sad. Romantic, I would say."

"We tend not to call it sad."

"No? Not so? I read this in a book—'the religion of the broken heart'—is it not aptly said?"

"Well, but wait a minute," I put in, "that's too much." I was speaking over noise and glare. The fact that I couldn't make out his face was beginning to bother me. I walked over and shut the window, drawing the shade partway down. Better. From the rectory grounds, I could still hear Mike Vaught, our sacristan, hammering away loudly at something, I couldn't think what. *One-TWO, one-two-three-FOUR*—it was getting to me: a semaphore of reproach. More than once during the past week Mike had interrupted my conference with a visitor by creating one kind of noise or another.

"Sorry—what were you saying?" I asked, resettling.

" 'The religion of the broken heart' . . . the faith of the beautiful failure," Mr. Adab resumed. I'd heard him right the first time.

"A Christian wouldn't think of it in those terms," I cautioned him.

"A Christian—a twice-born Christian—wrote this book!"

"I'd like to know *who*—" I broke in, the soul of orthodoxy suddenly. I was surprised to hear myself. Then, more calmly, I tried to explain. "We think beyond the cross to the resurrection, you see. Resurrection is the very heart of our faith. Death is not the last word for us, the story is not finished there. By no means."

He sniffed, took out a handkerchief, unfolded it, dabbed it to his nose and the corners of his mouth, then refolded it into fourths. He said with a little sadness, "I see you do not believe me."

I protested that I did. I didn't doubt that he'd read this somewhere.

"I am too blunt, perhaps . . ."

"I'd like to see the whole passage—to understand the full context," I said.

We parted politely enough. He promised to send me the citation, chapter and verse, and I fully expect to find it in the mail one of these days. It doesn't matter who said it, though. It's a mistake, a misunderstanding.

In the meantime, while I wait for Mr. Adab to check his sources, I dream about him. He's only one of a crowd, a long procession of passengers and next-of-kin, passing through the numbered gate, entering the boarding tunnel, that horn of silence. Then, still in silence, leaving the tunnel, crossing a long stretch of apron to the waiting plane. And there he is—I spot him—my Moslem inquisitor. He's lagging a few steps behind the others.

Then he's waving to me. I think so. A wave, or some gesture of parting. I must be at the window, inside, while watching this, but can't be because of what comes next. Maybe I am, though, doubly—magically—placed, at once inside and outside, in that curious way that spectators are positioned in dreams. It's all so still, but not because of the glass, there's no glass between them and me, I'm sure of that.

They're mounting the ramp, the last steps. Now they're filing into the passenger cabin. It's huge. I'm closing in, running or zooming—camera, mind's eye, coming in close —this big jet shape, the wings sleeked back. There are no engines, fore or aft.

I've had this dream twice and each time wakened

abruptly, heart pounding, at the same place. Right here: somebody racing, running hard—a last straggler, racing to catch up with them. See how he runs! Faces darken the porthole windows, gazing out. He's tearing across the tarmac, late, but not too late—

It's me—I'm almost there—there's something I've got to tell them—

That's when I wake up.

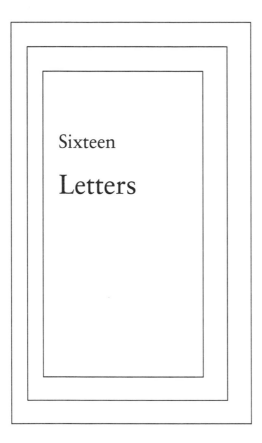

Sixteen

Letters

I WAS BACK at my post. The central post office in Hardesty had made up a stamp for me, so I set to work on all the sacks of mail that had been stuffed into the cargo bay of the plane. I had to interrupt for dusting and sweeping as I went along—flakes of ash kept falling over everything. Even after I'd swept, the air was so thick I could hardly breathe and I had to keep opening my window, chilly as it still was. The stamp said: DAMAGED IN AIR ACCIDENT, but the damage was as much from rescue operations as from the accident itself, as much from water-spotting as from scorching. Some of the mail seemed to be untouched; I sent those things quickly on their way.

Soon as I'd laid by our local mail, Francie Alred stopped in wanting some forwarding forms. Francie's a touchy one —she's never been real warm or friendly. She went off looking for fame and fortune; now she's back, no husband, and I can't say I didn't see it coming. She's one of those new women doing without men.

What else new? Chip spoke to me this morning. That's somewhat of an event. Only long conversation I ever had with him was years ago. He'd been gone for nearly a week and Cindy Bonner, who lived up the road from the Parkers, and needed help with her lawn, had come by day after day asking for him. When Chip finally turned up, I put it to him. "You shouldn't go off alone," I told him. "I wasn't alone," he said, "I had my dog with me." "A dog's not a person," I said to that. But Chip disagreed: "To me, he is." And that was that—our longest discussion ever.

Reason he came in this morning was to send back one of those free first offers. He wanted to make sure he wouldn't get charged for it. It was a wilderness book, from a club that aimed to make him a subscriber. Can't imagine how they happened on his name. He's got a driver's license, so I guess he reads, however barely. Wasn't so long ago, I recall one of his teachers telling me how it was a waste of time and paper keeping him in school, even trying to pretend to teach him to read and write, he was so far behind. That same summer, I saw him standing at the side of the road, selling potatoes. He was thirteen or fourteen, his uncle had just passed on; the sign said POTOS, the most mournful shaky strands for letters— all but the O's, he could do circles—but I thought, for sure, he'd never make it.

It's a marvel he talks at all. For years, he didn't, and we thought he was simple. Simple, or deaf. He'd be running around near naked like some cedar-chopper's kid, half wild, till the neighbors stepped in. We donated a heap of clothing and somebody must of dressed him; he started looking a whole lot more decent. It was after that he started in jabbering. There were things he wanted, I guess, and the best way of getting them was to name them. I'd always said he wasn't slow—only, somehow, *gripped*—

He never did warm to anyone, though. I don't remember when exactly he started raising dogs, but it seems to do well for him. He's easier with animals than with people, that I do know. He's perfectly polite—it's all "Miss Wootens" and "Ma'ams" when he talks to me but, today as before, he never says much. Then I learned he'd gotten a new stud dog since Buck died. "That's good, Chip," I said. "I'm sure he'll work out."

"Hope so."

People say Chip's shaken since the accident. Maybe. I couldn't see much of a change, myself. Of course, it was much too quick of a conversation to judge. I heard he had a run-in with the law on the day of the crash and got slapped around some. Nobody would tell me what for. "Don't ask," Jim Titus advised, "believe me, you don't want to know." I told Jim that I liked to be the judge of what I do and do not want to know. "Trust me,

Glenna, on this," he said. But there's no point sparing me, to my way of thinking. Sooner or later, *everything*—from that plane and everything else—comes into the light of day.

Geneva Wilson hasn't changed one whit, that's clear. It's the same old same old. She arrived six minutes before closing time, wouldn't you know it, when my hands were tied tallying up for the day. *What now?* She was toting a canary in a cage. "It's the Eye-rainians," she announced, "terrorists—" Her theory of the crash, I suppose.

Geneva's semi-deaf; she can hear a ring but not a knock, you never know what's getting through for sure. So I wasn't about to start up with her on anything but business—and that, fast. I leaned over the counter and raised my voice. "What can I do for you today, Geneva?" I asked, bracing myself.

She swung the cage up to the counter. That done, seems like she clean forgot whatever it was had brought her in. Like it flew out of her head. She tried patting her hair, which was ratted up on top, but her hand shook so it just made lace in the air.

Then she recollected: the canary was to be sent off to her niece in Wellington. She wanted the cheapest way. "That would be parcel post," I said. Turned out—no surprise to me—that she hadn't enough money for it. Geneva rarely has two nickles to click together. "I could loan it to you, Geneva," I suggested. Well, she raised up on that! "I don't take charity," she answered, testy. "A loan's not charity," I said, but she'd quickened at the very mention of the word. "Lemme see that again," she said. So I placed the cage on the scale yet again and read off the weight a second time. Same thing, coming to seventy-three cents over what she had. "I don't believe that scale for one minute," she declared, and commenced fanning the cage with one hand, fluffing and ruffling the air till the poor creature hopped off his perch and fluttered a little on its cramped wings. "Look again!" Geneva said, so I did and—still don't believe it!—the weight was lessening, an ounce for every wing beat, I swear!

"I'll take charge of it, Geneva," I said. "This'll do nicely." I scooped up the change she'd poured on the counter. "I'll have to wrap it now."

One thing about Geneva—she never went to charm school. She went off grumbling, "I don't take charity, never have. Never." And, soon as she'd closed the door behind her, I started laughing to myself, first time in a long while.

Coming up the driveway to the house, I saw a car parked at the edge of the field. It was one of the airport-rented cars, I'd seen enough of them to know. Fathers, mothers, children, spouses, cousins, friends . . . They come unannounced, walk, stand, stare out, clutter my fence with wreaths, and sometimes messages—notecards wedged into the plastic leaves. There's no way those cards can be permanently affixed. They blow off, and I gather them and tack them up again, never knowing which belongs where. Does it matter, really? They're all the same message: *Missing you . . . Dearest . . . Loved, Remembered, Longed for always . . .* Then some in languages I don't know, don't even know the letters to the words. But

I bet they say the same things. Same handful of phrases the world over is what I'm coming to believe.

This man, this new visitor, was weeping into one hand and gripping the fence post with the other. He looked like one of the Asians. Come from God knows how far away.

I jammed on the brakes soon as I spotted him, thinking maybe I'd back out for a little bit and wasn't there something I forgot to pick up at the grocer's. Ketchup!—I was short on ketchup. I don't like to intrude. But he must of heard me: he straightened, and I had to move forward. Coming closer, I waved. He stared right through me.

If I come upon them and they seem to want to talk, I talk, and sometimes I invite them in for a cup of coffee. If they want to be left alone, I let them be. This one, I left.

Shutting the door on myself, it was different than before. No matter what room I was in, I didn't feel any privacy. Felt like the walls had ears. Eyes, too, so help me.

The crash inspectors were gone. They were still puzzling it out, would be at it for months, but they'd gleaned the field to their satisfaction. Some machinery had been sent over to scrape off the topsoil, then a bulldozer to turn the soil over. How long does it take to replenish topsoil? Sixty years an inch? Nobody knew how far those chemicals had seeped. There'd be no crop from Hannah's field this year, that was the only thing for sure. I'd been officially informed by letter that I'd be compensated for all damages. "Compensate"—that was their word. Same word they'd used to the families of the victims. Meaning: "to make up for." As if anything could—

"It'll be—better be—a bunch of money," Jim Titus said

to me. "There are lawyers that specialize in this, if you want to go that route." I didn't want to mess with lawyers, though, not if I could help it.

After the dozer was done, I was thinking of letting the grass take over for a season. It would cover the bareness, at least, and give visitors something nicer to look at.

I could never get away from the crash, though. Evenings after the news, I'd sort through more letters. I called them "letters" because that's how I read them. Like they'd been addressed to me personally. Telling me something somebody wanted me to know. Once in a while, not often, it's a real letter. Like this one:

> *Dearest—dearly invented,*
> *The foolishness train has gone, my kind of*
> *good spirits, and here*

And here—nothing—
It's nobody's letter now.

Mostly, they're nothing more than scraps of things—a bunch of tattered cocktail napkins with the Maxim logo, a blackened baseball card, a list of batting averages—all the light little bits of paper that the crash investigators missed and the wind turned up. I gather in the scraps, reading over what's in English, then bundle them up in a manila envelope. When the batch gets sizable, I send it off to an address I've been given.

It's the ones from the children that really get next to me. This one, I found out by the shed. A homework assignment from the looks of it. I'm judging from the ruled paper, the eraser smudges. The pained neatness.

Last time in class we learned about the heart and its chambers. We learned about the need of many valves.

Then there's this drawing—speckled with oil, but the colors still bright. It's of a house, boxy, with smaller boxes for windows and a door nested inside it, a corkscrew of black smoke twisting out the chimney. There's a band of bright blue running across the top of the page, the way little kids do sky—a lid, not an atmosphere. Don't know why it is kids always draw it that way, even out here where the sky sweeps right down to your feet.

Sometimes I find documents, official documents, like this vaccination certificate from Karachi, Pakistan. It's got stamps for yellow fever, cholera, and smallpox. I imagine it's for a man. No telling by the name, though, never heard the like. If he's alive, this man—or whoever—will need this.

Here's a travel agency receipt. Part of a page from what looks like a time-and-expense log. A vacation photo, over-exposed, of a not-so-young woman at the beach, standing in a swimsuit too short for her, cocking her hip and smiling, trying to look hopeful.

This one, I found tangled in a mess of baling wire. It's A.A., I believe, one of the twelve steps: *We admitted that we were powerless over alcohol—that our lives had become unmanageable . . .* The card's pretty well thumbed, pretty well frayed, but not from being caught up in the wire.

Some of it's a puzzle. This page, from a book:

> *I wish I could afford to keep a horse.*
> *I wish I knew.*

So do I with all my heart.
I wish you knew.
I would that all the world knew.

Never in my life have I heard anybody say "I would that the whole world knew." But it's English, from a book on learning English, I guess. There are funny-looking words like *het bekostigen* printed in pencil on the margin. And *laten wachten.* Sounds like somebody talking with a wooden spoon, or maybe a heavy piece of dental equipment, crammed between his teeth.

This last, I could of picked up anywhere. It's from some fortune-vending machine, advising the best time for investment, love, and travel.

How does it all add up? I ask, and I tell myself it doesn't. Why should it? But maybe it does. One thing I do know: these people, all of them, were busy with plans. They were planning on living.

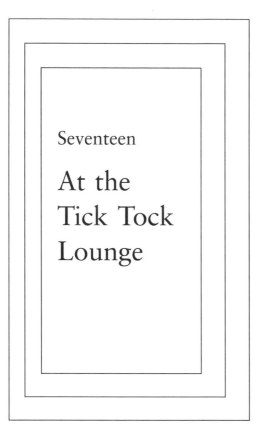

Seventeen

At the Tick Tock Lounge

SO HERE I WAS, same bar, same booth in same bar, same time nearly two weeks later, sitting by myself with the same pitcher of fresh draw in front of me, busy eavesdropping, same as before. The man from St. Louis was gone, and his lady listener, and most of the newcomers that blew in with the crash. Juanita and Francie were waiting on tables, helping out. There was a big racket just a moment ago; both television sets were going: some sort of game show with gongs, lots of clapping, and a blond woman in a long gown, spotted with golden spangles, jumping up and down. Two gongs, two jumping blondes, double spangles, every damned thing twice. Nobody was paying attention and Whitney lifted his remote and killed it.

I still hadn't actually gotten me a new stud dog, but I'd lined up a good prospect. I wasn't rushing into it, I guess, out of respect for Buck.

Up at the bar, somebody was talking cars. Engine problem. There was some discussion about his particular trouble. A rod knock was the verdict. Somebody else mentioned how he'd seen the rescue squad using grappling hooks to take out the last of the bodies from the passenger cabin, then he glanced around quick, case anybody from the passengers' families might of been here visiting with us. That wasn't likely, though.

There'd been whole bunches of relatives bussed over from the Dallas-Fort Worth airport since the crash. Seems like all those people had in mind was the one thing: getting themselves out to Miss Wooten's field to see for themselves where the plane went down. From time to time, I'd pass some of them moving slowly down Longview Street. They weren't working, shopping, or window-shopping; you couldn't miss who they were.

Anyhow, these people at Tick Tock were different. My guess is they had something to do with the press or television—the last ones to leave. They were drinking Dr Peppers and beers, and snacking on things. Three in the forward booth, two in the other behind it—woman woman man, man woman—talking amongst themselves in each booth, but not over the booth dividers. I was sitting across from that row of booths, so they were in my full view.

They'd been complaining about the quality of everything. "What do you call these sandwiches—'*pre-made*'?" one of the women in the forward booth grumbled. If Whitney heard, he didn't let on.

It was a little bit strange. You tend to think of all outsiders—specially Yanks, like these seemed to be—as coming from the same Yank town, and thinking the same Yank thoughts. I know I do. But the ones in the forward booth hadn't said pip to the ones in the booth behind them. Then—*wham!*—they connected. One of them must of overheard—something. Before I knew it, one lady had popped her head over the high back of the booth dividing them. "Excuse me," she said, "you're talking about the Tarrytown Hunan, aren't you?"

"How'd you know?"

"I don't believe it—we must be neighbors! I'm from New York, too—Pleasantville. It's the only decent Chinese restaurant for miles around."

"Tarrytown Chicken, Happy Family, and Buddha's Delight are our favorites. And the three-meal deal that goes for four."

"I don't *believe* it! Those are my favorites, too. My name's Gloria, by the way." She was the one who'd started it. The names went back and forth, a regular sing-along, and soon enough there they were, all five of them squeezed into one booth, spouting away "oh when? you're kidding!"—shit like that. They'd moved on from Chinese restaurants to dentists, how none of them could be trusted.

Who cares?

Time for a station break; I tuned them out. Nothing much else happening so I sort of drifted back to Miss Wooten's place; a rerun: me roving through that field, gliding along so sweetly I knew I was only sightseeing in my mind. Ground's edgy as a case of knives; but I'm dancing along, feet just tickling as I go. On past the wing all blown to kingdom come, the blue cap with the neat gold braid, the lady dolled up for a party, still strapped to her chair, still awaiting for it. Keep on keeping on, loping along . . . Then *whoa!*—backing up sharp, stumbling—I've stumbled on that hand—

So, enough, I quit—back to eavesdropping again. They were talking dreams: it was more interesting now.

"I dreamed I died. I'd been shot between the eyes, then I woke up. I felt wonderful."

"I never can remember my dreams," piped the one who called herself Gloria.

"I dreamed I was dreaming and I woke up, but my waking was also in the dream. I was standing in a shop window, stark staring naked—"

"I've had the same dream!"

I dreamed that skylab was falling. And that was no dream. I dreamed I was drinking muddy water from a ditch . . . I was drifting again. Plenty of words flying through the air, but they didn't add up. Somebody said, "Caught the nicest springer of bass," and somebody else kept breaking in with "What I'm saying is . . . *Right,* but what I'm saying is . . ."

Then they started chatting up the crash—I knew they'd get round to it eventually. "No rhyme of reason," said old

Jack Henderson. Andy Pearson disagreed. "When your time is up, it's up," he said, "don't matter what you do, whether you fly or go by mule. Heard there was a lottery winner on board, some lady, I believe from Selma, Alabama, riding first class to New York City. She'd only become a millionaire a couple months back. She was just starting to enjoy it—"

"I've never won anything." It was that lady, Gloria, from Pleasantville, again. The one who'd never dreamt anything either.

"Win one—lose one," said Whitney. "It's all a lottery."

The people from Gloria's booth began disputing the millionaire story. "Out-and-out untrue," one of them said, "nothing but rumor. That was checked out some time ago." According to them, the lottery winner never did get on board. She'd changed her flight at the last minute.

"Oh, well, then—win *two!*" said Whitney. "Talk about luck! Only goes to prove my point: it's all one big wheel of fortune. Blind chance." Then—all of a sudden—Whitney turned on me. "Love to have Chip's opinion on it." Backstabbing: "Chip was there. On the scene—"

Don't do this.

"Looks to me like Chip got snake-bit."

Don't look up.

"Too bad we can't all be so free-flowing," Whitney blatted on. "It's the great Parker chill-out, Chip's way of telling me to get lost." I stared at the table in front of me, the damp circle print of a glass, my fingers smushing the circle. Whitney went right on: "They call it an 'act of God' —that means nobody can explain it. No known motive."

Might of been a speech he'd prepared for. "I say you don't *have* to explain it. Don't even bother to try. It's all numbers, all there is to it. A wild throw of the dice. That's just my personal opinion, but nothing ever happened to convince me any different. It's scary, really, when you think of it. Everything, everybody, chancing along. But I sure would love to know what Chip thinks about it—"

"Lay off, Whitney!" It was Francie butting in. "Will you lay off for once?"

Chant to myself how I usually do—*he says she says it says* . . .

Keep my head down—*hear nothing, see nothing, say nothing. Be nothing.* That hand against my hand is all I'm thinking. Won't ever be free of it—

Eighteen

Recap

"WHY DON'T YOU go on along home, Francie?" Whitney urged. "Nothing but slack till closing time now. Bundle up and get going—"

Only one boothful of beer drinkers left, and the party there was winding down. Juanita, Whitney, and I were all sitting, enjoying a little respite. Whitney was smoking, Juanita filing her fingernails. She'd haystacked her hair: it was still standing up, a good five inches from her scalp, don't ask me how. I was doing nothing but metabolizing the air and staring—something Chip likes to do—down at the tabletop, at a cluster of cigarette scars in the corner of it, wondering whether they'd been put there on purpose. Less than half an hour to quitting time. Like Whitney said, the need was over. But I couldn't seem to rouse myself. Instead, I sat on while Juanita started lining up the different nozzles, brushes, and scoops, uncoiling the vacuum cord and wheeling the ancient Hoover out of the closet. Why *not* get going?

I dreaded the late drive home, for one thing, and, for another, I wasn't in the nicest of moods. I still had one honey of a headache—the aftermath of the cold or low-grade flu I'd just been through. And I was somewhat pissed. Royally pissed, if the truth be known. The way the people from the television crew or newspaper, or whatever, had been staring at us for days on end now. *Losers . . . not too many smarts*—I knew what they'd been thinking—*why would anybody live here otherwise?*

I was heartily sick of being a curiosity. That man with the camera, who came traipsing in after most of the reporters left, really was the last straw. It wasn't his job or anything, he hadn't that excuse. He'd been on the flight that went down, survived it without a scratch, and wanted a record, he told me, something to show his grandkids in days to come. He'd started out at the Wooten place, naturally enough, then roamed around shooting wheatfields and windmills, picking up on what he called "local color" —the elevator, town hall, *Home of Dan Lutes* sign, Brother Pipes's church, and finally, for no reason I could fathom, Kehoe Seed and Feed. At Kehoe, he'd latched on to me. He kept rummaging a hand through his thin hair and saying, "I must've been spared for some reason—what could it be?" I confessed I couldn't help him there, then mumbled something polite about hoping he'd find out before long. Then he asked about me, how long I'd been working in the seed business, and whether I'd lived anywhere besides Bounds.

"Dallas . . . Chicago . . . St. Louis . . . New York . . ." I rattled off the names. His face! The look on his face. "And you came back—*here?*" he said. "City too much for you?"

"You better believe it!" I cut him off. I didn't say: *too much and too little.* Didn't mention that I'd *chosen* to come back; it's hard enough getting anybody here to believe it. "Came back licking her wounds" is the official version of it in Bounds, I'm sure. Nobody says it to my face, but . . .

And I'm sure they all say they saw what was coming ages and ages ago. Growing up in Bounds, it was no secret that I couldn't wait to be gone. Anybody with ambition felt the same way, though they might not have publicized it top of their voices, way I did. Another thing different in my case—I wasn't pining for romance, whatever that might be. I knew I wasn't built for it. And I wasn't thinking marriage, either. There was absolutely no inspiration for it on the local scene, to start with, and I'd never bought the idea of dying into peace, the dead-to-yourself-but-all-alive thing that I'd been taught was the secret of womanly success. I'd seen a whole procession of women going that way—Lazelle Post, Glenna Wooten, my great-aunt Alma—a whole generation. All of them fretting themselves to death trying to please everybody. And nobody pleased. I'd seen them baking up a storm, trying to sweeten, to prettify everything. It's a wonder we aren't all diabetic!

I wasn't blaming anyone—I'd done what I resolved to do. I'd set out to seek my fortune, like they say in the old fairy tales. Whatever happened, I'd learn for myself what was what. I had. I'd come back from all my plans of making a name for myself—pianist, program notes editor, programmer, marketing researcher—I'd had my fill of hustling. I'd been in such a desperate hurry to make things happen, to leave an imprint. What was it all about? Hard to even imagine now. Here, the only imprints are plow cuts, and only for a season. And the only mirror is sky.

One of the first things I did when I got back was to make a list. Double columns: *What I Want* on the left; *What I'm Going to Get* on the right. Only place where right and left columns matched was on the first item— what I wanted most. That was *standability:* I wanted to "acquire standability," as my father used to say of a promising crop, and I thought I might actually achieve it in a hard place like Bounds. Then I wrote *not much variety* on the right. But I'd had variety aplenty where I'd been. There'd been too many shops in too many cities and I'd wanted everything. Everything, and nothing. There was nothing in them I wanted. I'd be in a department store, gazing round at blushers, eyeshade, perfume bottles, lingerie, silk scarves and whatnot, seeing myself reflected in a million mirrors, the winking, glittering lights of appe-

tite, and I'd freeze, couldn't move a muscle. I'd be standing there, my mouth working, no sound coming out, looking like the yokel I was. I was gaping with hunger—
hunger for nothing I could name . . .

Juanita had finished, and Whitney was swabbing down
the counter for the umpteenth time—his last. The last customers were at the door. It was so quiet I could hear a
motor gunning in the back lot, and a cattle truck, heavy-
laden, rumbling down the Interstate, a lone steer, mouth
pressed to the slats, bellowing as he went, bleat after bleat,
like a trailing banner.

There were a lot more people on their own in Bounds
since I'd gone away . . . Widows rattling around in big
old houses that used to be crowded and cozy. And, sure,
we'd had them always—a full share of oddballs, loners,
losers. A maverick like Chip who needs a lot of space,
who jumps out of his skin if you come up too close behind
him, wouldn't be able to get by anywhere else. That teas-
ing business tonight—Whitney ought to know better.
Chip won't be pried out, ever, though it's always tempting
to try to. Only human to want to know his slant on
things. He's always listening and not saying. If you wait
and watch real quietly, you can catch him out laughing to
himself, or saying things behind locked teeth. But you'll
never really know what he's thinking. I say, leave him be.
Maybe keep an eye out for him.

Then I did something I've never done before. I was beat,
near bow-legged with weariness, but I staggered onto my
feet, and lugged myself up to the tap. Poured out a glass of
beer. This one for me. Half a glass, really, half air; I raised

a nice tall head of foam on it. "To peace and quiet," I said, holding the glass aloft.

"Amen to that," said Whitney, "for a couple hours, at least." Then he added: "I guess you've come home, Francie," and I heard myself saying: "I guess."

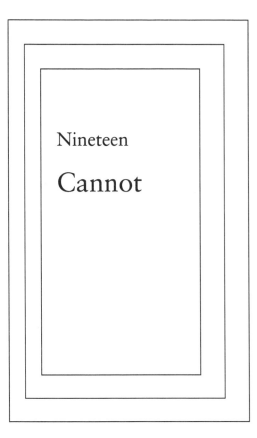

Nineteen

Cannot

FIRST LIGHT. No colors yet no lines. Only zones . . .
shadings of a monochrome. The thread-end of a dream
. . . Can't catch it.

This morning's mantra: *Let live.* Say it softly. Again. It's
so quiet I can hear the small bones of my neck turning,
eyelids lifting. I *don't* want to get up.

Shadows loosening . . . Landmarks: Bureau. Chair.
Bed table. Inlets between . . . The long arm of the cruci-

fix, arrowed at the ceiling. It's that other arm, across—the wide, stretched arms—they're forgetting, they keep on forgetting—What's this about "sweet stalks"?

There it goes: the old digital clicking into action. Six-o-what? Missed it. "Moisture-wise we're doing well." Soil temperature: thirty-seven degrees six inches down. How about temperature above the soil? Must have just missed it. Damp and chill, my bones tell me. Daily Mass at seven, coming right up. I'm more or less awake, I will get up. But no point rushing couple minutes yet . . . How's that? "Cows steady to firm . . ." No small feat in this shifting world.

How about it?

Couple minutes yet . . . Livestock reports: cattle . . . feeder cattle . . . light choice boxed beef, heavier choice, light selects, heavier selects . . . Futures: hogs . . . April live feeders, May pork bellies.

More numbers, a litany of numbers: wheat, grain sorghum, corn, cotton. Soybeans, oats. The sound logo—a mournful radio cow honking—for Wiggins Used Cow Dealers, a rendering company offering free dead stock removal. *Enough*—

Radio off, I sat on the edge of the bed, bare feet to the bare floorboards, soaking up the rawness. The chill. I reached for the breviary on my bedside table and rested my hand on the cover for a moment. No use praying this morning. Besides, I was late—six twenty-four—time to be up and about. Get *with* it—make the motions!

I nicked myself shaving, and the memory I'd been steering clear of swept over me in one fast wash—Mike Vaught and Tom Steen chanting almost in unison: "Whose church is this, anyway?" I dabbed at the cut with styptic and there I was, back at the parish council meeting last night, the burble of the coffee machine and small talk in the background—the usual warming-up sounds. Finances were on the agenda, my least favorite subject, best handled by Tom Steen who's a CPA. High on the list was the utility bill, this past month an all-time high.

Everybody agreed that heavy weather accounted for some of the increase. "But there's another thing, Father . . ." a small cough, and Tom launched into it. My recent practice of leaving the church open at all hours had clearly contributed to rising costs. And, while he was at it: how much extra time had I been devoting to strangers lately? Judging from Tom's composure, and the way the others were sitting—eyes shuttered, heads piously downcast—he wasn't alone in his views.

It still rankled. The time issue was none of their concern; it was *my* spare time. Time added onto all the usual things. I let them know this. I tried to say something, too, about the relatives of the victims who'd been coming to me to talk about their loved ones, or to pause a moment at Blessed Redeemer, people coming from immense distances, called out by the crash.

"All very well to say, Father." Tom sighed. "The next question is: who's going to pay for this?" And then, in chorus, Tom, Mike, and another voice: "Whose church is this, anyway?" I had to excuse myself before blurting out something I'd regret later. I delegated George Swanson for the closing prayer and walked stiffly to the door, trying to contain myself. "Save souls, Padre" was Mike Vaught's parting shot.

It stung me, even now. Slapping cold water on my cheeks did nothing to moderate it.

The sacristy was empty—no sign of Pete, the kid who's supposed to be my altar server on Wednesday mornings. There's a pattern, I decided: Pete must wake with the light; clouded mornings, he can't be counted on. I'd managed without him before, though.

My hand was on the hanger. I had every intention of going through with the scheduled Mass, same as every morning. I would give thanks, bless the bread, break it, and share it. I touched the alb, *No.* Too angry. Too narrow a sharing. I tried my mantra—*let live.* Now. And again. It wasn't working. an empty wire hanger clattered to the floor. They were waiting for me, my daily communicants, they were not to blame. I stooped to retrieve the fallen hanger. Blood rushed, scalding, to my face. *No.* I didn't want to hear their *alleluias* and *amens,* their *kingdom comes.* Couldn't make the little ceremonies of crossing and blessing, of chalice and veil. And surely not the great gestures. Couldn't lift the bread or the cup. Not this morning.

Nearly seven.

I turned then, out of the sacristy, out the back door of the church and followed the muddy footpath around to the front entrance. I guess it was raining lightly: thinking back on it later, I wasn't sure. I had no recollection of my feet moving, or of mounting the front steps, entering the vestibule—nothing. Until I arrived at the door. I stood on the threshold as a passerby—a stranger—might, wondering: *Who are these people? What are they about?*

Quiet inside: a votive candle jittering in the draft; a rosary tapped wood. They all sat in their coats. A decision on the heating must have been made last night after I walked out. I could smell the wool, the thin, sour dampness, through the drenching sweetness of the flowers, the heaps of flowers our visitors persist in bringing. They were sitting so far apart from one another that they seemed to be praying at separate altars. From the backs of their heads, I could call them by name: Mary Ward. Amy Pote. Loyd Winders. Chris Brenan. Sady and Mary Grimes. Wayne Gruver. In the chill, I imagined their prayers clumped in little cloud captions, one hovering above each head. There was no mingling.

I don't know how long I stood there. Probably not very, but it seemed long. It was almost perfectly quiet now, yet I felt as though I stood at the ear of a wind tunnel. Heads turned as I moved down the aisle. Not a word was said, but I knew I had their attention.

I didn't try to reach the pulpit. Standing between the first pew and the altar steps, I began without preamble. "I'm sorry"—no need to project my voice—"I cannot celebrate Mass this morning."

A teachable moment, maybe, but I was much too churned up to teach. They sat on, unmoving, waiting for more, but there was nothing I could add to what I'd said. My throat seized up—the word clotted in my throat:

"Can-not."

They lingered for some minutes after I left—a little stunned, I'm sure—while I waited, also shaken, leaning against the sacristy wall, eyes closed, ears ringing. "Hear me out!" I breathed. But who was stopping me now?

When I heard the kneelers folding into place, the shuffling of feet, and the first words blurred in passage, I knew it was over. Only then did I move on to my office and some semblance of my normal day.

The Grimes sisters were waiting for me in the corridor. I waved them into my office, but they remained standing on the threshold. "We won't be staying," Sady said gently. "Just came to ask, are you ill, Father?" It was a way out she was offering me. I might have taken it—I had not been kind. I regretted that. But I could do no other.

"No"—I was firm on this—"my health isn't the issue." I promised to explain when I could—some other time. That didn't slow Sady down for a minute. "I'll pray for you, Father," she said. I thanked her, automatically; it would take more than prayer. What I needed, for a start, was to take a long walk around everyone. Around the church, several times. A long walk around myself, too.

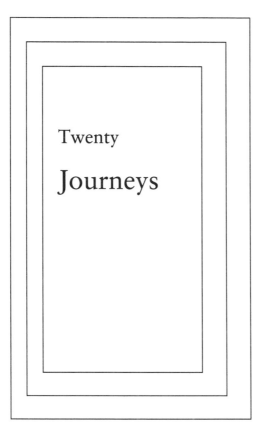

Twenty

Journeys

SOME PEOPLE at Blessed Redeemer still don't get it. Worse—they've started a whispering campaign. Rumors abound. I caught wind of the most vicious of them only last week—a wild fantasy about one of the visitors removing our best chalice from the sacristy and using it in some sort of satanic rite, then returning it, neatly polished and desecrated, to its usual place, ready for our use. In fact, the chalice has never strayed from its cupboard in the sacristy; Mike Vaught and I are the only ones who have a key. I denounced the story in ringing tones from the pulpit, but rumor has a life of its own and I doubt we've heard the last of it. In the meantime, I go about my usual business of ritual and encounter and begging for funds. Three members of the parish council have resigned. They've threatened to write a letter to the bishop concerning the high cost of my policy of unlimited hospitality. The letter will also mention my refusal to say Mass the morning after our last parish council meeting. It will be meant sincerely and signed "sincerely in the names of Jesus, Mary, and Joseph," and will stress its sole concern for the welfare of Holy Mother Church. Let them write it. Many such letters are written to chancery offices. Let the bishop call me in. I am equally sincere. I'm not backing down on this.

Mike Vaught and a couple of others on the parish council are in the habit of referring to our new visitors as "outsiders" or "strangers." I persist in referring to them as "neighbors"—distant neighbors called out, and brought close, by calamity—I seem to be stuck on this way of speaking. These visitors have come to Bounds, to us, and I, at least, have to be here to receive them. It isn't always pleasant or easy. Often, I don't know the first thing. There are so many languages, and I don't have the grammar books, the customs-of-the-country guides, not to mention the liturgical rubrics, to cover the case before me. All I can do is to listen, and gesture from time to time. To be present. That doesn't sound like a whole lot, yet, with these visitors, I've had little uncertainty about my calling. It's curious: no rubrics, no maps—fewer doubts. Of course, there wasn't much time for reflection at first, but there is now. Even if I can't put a ready name to it, I don't question my usefulness. It's as if, late in my career, I'd found my vocation, or confirmed it, or fitted into it, at last. It's been a long and winding road I've traveled.

What Father Fogarty saw in me that day I barged into his rectory, three decades ago in Windy, I still can't figure. Even at the time, I sensed what a mishmash of motives had drawn me to his door. Part of it, I'm sure, was simply impatience to break free from the confines of family and too-small town. But there was more to it than that: something to do with girls and guns and hellish laughter. It was part longing—sexual beckoning, part fear, part pride, with some hungering for righteousness, for meaning, some vague yearning for a peaceable kingdom thrown in.

And I can't say I had it sorted out by the time my ordination day came. Talk about nervous! I'd fasted that morning, and the day before as well; I put it down to hunger that everything seemed so unreal. The lamps flickered and faded, part of the perishing world, near and far seemed equally faint and far, the very walls seemed to desubstantiate before my eyes. My mother's face, the path I followed down the central aisle to the altar, the rising smoke of the censer, the bishop's miter (shaped so curiously like the open mouth of a fish!) . . . none of it seemed familiar. Of course, the bishop was a fisher of men. I'd been, as he put it, "called out from among men." As I prostrated myself before the altar, before bishop and priests, before my bewildered parents and the members of my home parish, as I stretched out to my full length, face to the floor like something slain, I felt myself being drawn slowly upright, a strange fish out of the depths, into a fog of incense, of clabbered, unbreatheable air. "He now belongs to all the people," said the bishop, "and his work takes him into your midst, to bless, to exhort, to console, to administer the sacraments, to bring God's peace." I would try, I would do my best—it seemed next to impossible, even then.

I thought the sense of strangeness would pass, that parish work would help set my feet on the ground. Little did I guess. In short order, I was commissioned and sent forth to St. Boniface in the town of Hopper. Hopper's out between Two Tree and Anson's Gap—not exactly a blooming metropolis. Not that much bigger than Bounds. But it wasn't the place that made this assignment so out of this world, so little likely to put earth under my feet; it was the pastor, Monsignor Engelbrecht.

He was a short man with immaculate white hair, a perpetually red face, and a habit of exclaiming, "Gosh, my!" when anything surprised him, and a great many things did surprise him. He had a wen, like a clouded tear, beneath his left eye—I don't know why I remember this.

Off hours, you'd find him either smoking or eating celery—to cut the bite of his pipe. He was a passionate pipe-smoker; as far as I could tell, smoking was his only vice. There wasn't much I *could* tell, really. He had such difficulty talking to me face to face that he often used his dog, an old terrier called "Soldier" as a go-between. "Soldier, would you please ask Father Mark to take the seven-thirty Mass tomorrow? . . . I wonder, Soldier, whether Father Mark remembered the second collection today?" Soldier's ears would perk up each time his name was mentioned.

There I'd be, at the same table, sitting face to face with the man.

He was very good with children, and had few problems with people in serious trouble, but normal adult conversation seemed beyond him. At the pulpit, he'd turn hoarse with stage fright, although he'd been preaching for more than fifty years. He read all his homilies from frayed, handwritten notes, without looking up from the page to the faces in front of him. Yet his parishioners made allowances for all his idiosyncracies, for his kind heart and ineptitude in practical matters. They called it "unworldliness" and would not have him change a thing.

Foolish, but harmless, I thought. His homilies were recycled every three years; I doubted whether he'd cracked a theology book in decades. Communion wafers were "the bread of angels—our passport to heaven." The frequent reception of Communion was not only for the spiritual nourishment of the soul, but also for the "lessening of concupiscence, preservation from mortal sin, forgiveness of venial sin, and strengthening against temptation." His themes were few, concupiscence and death always in the foreground. He believed that salvation was contained in the sacraments as water in a cup, and that we were saved one by one, a quantum a sip. His arms, when he raised the chalice, were vaulted straight to heaven.

"He means well" was my most generous assessment of Monsignor Engelbrecht. I had assumed that there was in him a certain closed smugness, a finality of folded hands but, towards the end of my term with the man, I began to suspend judgment. There were layers to him.

One night, passing his bedroom on the way to my own,

I noticed his door, usually shut by the time I went up to bed, now ajar. I spied the shank of an iron bedstead, a knitted blue cover. Soldier was already settled on a far corner of the bed; he pointed one ear as I slipped by. The old man had been kneeling, lost in prayer, but his hands weren't pressed together as I'd imagined; they were spread the length of the bed, his arms stretched out. He was making the sign of the cross with his entire body.

My second assignment was an altogether different case. Father Glimm, the pastor at St. Thomas in Bradley, had no difficulty looking me in the eye or telling me exactly what he thought. He was an enormous man, well over two hundred pounds—a man of dramatic moods, by no means always jolly. A great dissipater of what he dubbed "pious piffle"—he could detect it instantly in any and all forms. Directness was Father Glimm's strong suit. The first day of stewardship week he billed as "Give-a-Damn Sunday." A certain compulsive communicant, who was in the habit of receiving the Host and walking out the door, was "getting his fix"—Father Glimm had little patience for that kind of devotion. Only two kinds of people in the world, in his view: "light givers and obstructors of the light." Most people—he included himself in this category —were something of both. "Take my word for it," he said. I didn't, back then, but, more and more lately, I've been coming round to his way of seeing things.

Listening in on my preaching, Father Glimm was lavish with homiletic advice. "Better steer clear of the Trinity," he warned, "but if you feel you must, give it no more than three minutes. More than three and you're bound to be in heresy." When I tried to reflect on the human side of things, I fared no better: "What's this I hear you talking about? Your 'life experiences'? Please! When did you ever have life experiences?"

Yet, for all his crankiness, he was a very solid priest, and he'd been at it for over thirty-five years. Looking back on it, I think I needed Glimm and Engelbrecht both. Neither one of them alone would have given me a fair picture of the balancing act that most parish work requires—an impossible act, really. In addition to the usual infighting of any institution, we've got two churches, pre- and post-conciliar, tethered together, chanting together "one holy, catholic, and apostolic" and slugging it out with one another.

My troubles had not yet begun, though. I was still an associate through my next two assignments; the senior man bore the brunt of anything I stirred up. Then came the first church of my own: St. Agnes, in a suburb of Wichita Falls. Built only two years before, and already the parish was debt-free. Why this plum assignment fell to me, I'll never know. It was an altogether "tasteful" church, high-toned, rich, and cold, and my job was to change nothing, but simply go along with them and tend to the sacramental business. I put it cynically—I felt it that way. There, at St. Agnes, I was kept mindful of the political coloration of my homilies by the rise and fall of the Sunday collection. I began to feel like a hired manager, expected to please those who paid my hire. Like a *kept* man. It was clear to me then that serving had nothing to do with pleasing, and everything that's gone on since, including the recent rumblings in Bounds, has only strengthened that conviction.

St. Agnes had irked me from the start. Even the look of the place, statues and images banished for a sleek, ultra-modern effect, the crucifix clean-cut, unburdened, minus the Suffering Servant. I missed the Corpus. Resurrected without a pang is what that sanitized crucifix said to me. Again—not *my* idea of what our story's about. At parish council meetings, the burning issues were decorum, finances, litter, and how to keep youngsters from trampling the flower beds. What went on beyond the parking lot never came up, unless I forced it.

On Holy Thursday, kneeling to wash the cleanest feet in the parish, I wanted only to flee. I saw it through, though —from Holy Week to Easter, Easter to Pentecost, Pentecost to Ordinary Time. I moved in a tight daze. Evening after evening, I'd return to my plush rectory—a cocoon, if ever there was—and sink into torpor. Couldn't seem to lift myself from the La-Z-Boy armchair. When I finally did, and stretched out on the bed, I was unable to sleep. My lethargy seemed connected to my lodgings with their perfect temperature control and the prevailing numb atmosphere of that church, a sort of wraparound spiritual carpeting. For months I'd daydreamed of breaking out of the cocoon, of leaving everything I knew behind and hitting the open road. Of meeting life on its own terms at last.

I was suffocating. I had to go. I'd developed blinding headaches and—I had it in writing—"stress-related cardiovascular abnormalities." I'd visited two doctors, and ended up in the hospital, having taken both sets of prescriptions at once. So I had no choice; the diocese had no choice. A "vocation crisis" was the official name for what I suffered. "A year of discernment" was the remedy I sought. In my case, added to St. Agnes, there was the matter of adolescence, the one I'd missed, long postponed and overdue.

Part of my daydream involved boarding a bus and setting forth for an unknown destination. When the place was right, I'd know it and step off. Simply pull my suitcase off the bus and walk into town, a stranger. Start over, completely fresh.

I did board that bus, but not in the bright spirit of those ads for "See America" passes. Those turned out to be the most aimless weeks of my life. That awful summer I'd spent biking around in circles as a teenager was beautifully focused in comparison.

I disembarked in a number of towns, bearing steadily eastward. I'd hole up in a motel for a few days, walk the streets, then return to my cell, my solitary reading. That's what those motel rooms were—cells. There were few regional touches and, except for the scuff marks and stains, the stale, unexpungeable odors of cigarettes laced with Airwick, no traces of the lives passing through those rooms, no signatures.

The ironies were not lost on me. I'd broken out of the cocoon of parish life and here I was out in the world, leading a nearly enclosed life. Free—and, at the same time, entombed. Except for settling my bill or exchanging a few words with strangers at the ice machine, or a "how do!" to the girl with the clean-up cart, I didn't speak to a living soul. Once a day, I'd ask the woman who worked at the front desk whether there'd been any mail or messages for me, but, after three or four days, I'd become so predictable that she'd greet me with "nothing again!" the minute I cracked open the door.

Motel nights are long. When I couldn't sleep, I'd listen to toilets flushing, to doors opening and slamming shut. I'd follow the slow glide of headlights across the ceiling. Sometimes a couple would party or fight in the room next door, the woman usually shouting, "What do you take me for!" before it was over. Sometimes there'd be other sounds coming through, intimate words and noises I didn't think I ought to hear. Then I'd stuff my ears with toilet paper to drown them out. This magnified the sound of my own heart beating.

My money was running out when I left the bus in Frederick, Maryland. Why Frederick? I liked the look of the place, those old stonework houses. And somebody on the bus had mentioned a school for the deaf there.

Seeking employment in Frederick, I was reminded of just how unemployable I was. What, after all, were my special skills? Confecting the Eucharist—turning bread into Flesh, wine into Blood? Try mentioning that! Naturally, I didn't. I did have some experience in counseling, minus the crucial social work degree. I also had some knowledge of books and a few ancient languages, so I started out cataloging in a library, a temporary position. I rented a small furnished apartment close by. The apartment was only a little more personable than the motels I'd been frequenting. Working again was an improvement, though. I started to make friends, a woman among them.

A moment of truth started us off. The lunchroom was crowded; single diners were sharing tables. She asked if she could share with me. I said, "Sure," hardly glancing up from whatever it was I was reading or pretending to read. I expected silence or a smattering of small talk, but she battered my barricade of newsprint down, asking point-blank: "Are you lonely?" I must have simply stared back in silence, uncertain whether I'd heard her aright, for she asked again, "Would you like somebody to talk to?"

I startled myself by answering, "Very much." I didn't even recognize the voice in which I said it, a full register below my normal voice. And that was only the first surprise.

She was one of the reference librarians. I must have seen her in passing any number of times before that lunch, but I'd never paused long enough to notice. A tall girl, gracefully built, with dark hair foaming around a rather thin face. She was altogether generous, eager to please, and her face showed this, her smile going right up to the gums. Good to look at, if not outright beautiful. "Easy on the eyes" I believe is the expression. But nothing else was easy, nor could it have been, for me.

Soon we were eating lunch together as a rule; then, when that wasn't enough, we added on suppers—a progression. I was, as they say, "falling in love." The words are partly right: it was a fall. Whatever it was that started us off—friendliness, frankness, loneliness, curiosity—seemed innocent enough, but soon grew obsessive, as relentless, as monotonous, as any addiction. I began to brood over certain words she'd said and how they were said, the exact shading of her voice, the meaning of a glance, the way she filled the hours we spent apart, what she looked like when she slept, breasts, thighs, etcetera, etcetera, trying not to think about it, thinking about it,

picturing things, mind-movies that ran wild. And then—
they weren't movies, I wasn't brooding or dreaming, but
wide-awake. I felt shredded, shipwrecked—swept under a
breaking wave.

Skin to skin, we were farther apart than ever before. I
wanted to kneel by the side of that tangled bed and spread
my arms wide across it and beg for forgiveness, but only
sat in the midst of it, hugging my knees. "You did fine,"
she said to me. When I tried to apologize, she stared at
me, stricken. Then she took my hand. "It's nothing to be
sorry about," she spoke softly, putting her face close to
mine, as you would to a child. "Really," she said, "it's no
big deal." But it was for me. A very big deal, indeed.

We were careful with each other for the few days remaining after that. Within the same week, my mother
called with bad news.

Dad was in the hospital. "Since when?" I demanded to
know. There was a short spell of silence on the other end,
before she admitted the operation was over—"it had to be
done fast." They'd tried calling me, but I was never in.
"Anyway, it's over now. It's *done*. He's going to make it
—he's doing fine." A double heart bypass; he could have
died and I hadn't known. "The important thing is—when
are you coming?" she asked. "Soon as we're done talking," I promised. I knew I wouldn't be coming back.

It was unreasonable, I knew, it was wildly simplistic,
but I couldn't stop asking myself whether there wasn't a
connection between my actions and my father being
struck down right then. Pure coincidence, probably—no
meaning. But, sure, I could trot out some meanings, starting with the most obvious natural one—that it's all a mat-

ter of linked life cycles. Fact of nature: it's how the generations fit together. But I wasn't trained to act according to
nature. Not *first* nature, anyway.

Mercifully for all of us, Dad recovered without incident.
And I tried to be attentive and go more than halfway in
any argument with him after that. He died last year—
nothing to do with his heart. By then, we'd had time
enough to work through many things.

Back in the clerical fold, I led a probationary life, doing
office work at the chancery until reassignment time came
around. There were to be no more plum assignments for
me; I was sent out instead to aging country parishes, low-
budget holding operations, first in Slater, then Bolton. A
way of putting me out to pasture? I wondered about it
now and then, but didn't fret. I'd had my upscale parish
experience and it was not for me. It was after Bolton that I
came to Bounds.

Nothing in my training, or experience (I'd had *some* since
Father Glimm's day), had prepared me for the continuing
visits after the crash in Bounds. One afternoon on a day
that was simply a white space in the calendar, a day without a single saint tacked on to it, I entered my office to
retrieve some baptismal records. I thought I heard something stirring in the sanctuary, so decided to take a look. I
noticed a fresh batch of wildflowers scattered across the
steps to the altar, and made a mental note to gather them
and do them up more presentably. But nothing else was
out of place. No one about. Yet I kept on hearing something, some faint, worrying movement. Whenever I
paused, the sound trailed off, as though someone were

listening. But where? I made a rather self-conscious reverence as I passed the tabernacle—I *felt* watched—and made my way into one of the back pews. All quiet. I thought I might pray, or try to, and closed my eyes, the better to concentrate. Nothing came to mind but the nagging strain of my intention. I shaped the word "Father . . ." and, as if in echo, heard a voice whispering. Then, quite distinctly, the rustle of cloth. It was coming from the vestibule. I sprang to my feet and went after it.

And there it was—a woman crouching in the corner. Correction: not crouching, but kneeling, at a precise angle. I was reminded then that our narthex faced north by east, and it occurred to me that she was a Moslem. She was wearing some sort of Asian dress, all white. I withdrew as quickly as I'd come, but clumsily, beating a retreat back to my office, leaving the door open in case she wanted to visit with me after she was done. I hoped, fervently, that our sacristan was nowhere in the vicinity or I'd never hear the end of it.

Even with my door wide-open, she knocked and waited. I rose and beckoned her forward; she remained where she was, asking something. Directions, probably. "Please?" I said. All I could make out was "double you see"—a perfect conundrum, perfectly articulated. Her glance roved up and down the hall, so I hazarded a guess. "W.C. You want the water closet?" She affirmed this with a clear "thank you very much," and I pointed the way. I thought she might come by again on her way out—as she did.

I don't know how we got through the preliminaries, she had so little English. Her name was Shirazi—her surname, I assumed. I never caught her first name if she offered it.

From what I surmised, Mrs. Shirazi had lost a son in the crash. A son who lived with her and who may or may not have held a job. Who may have been in trouble. Or maybe this was another son still alive, still living with her. I couldn't be sure. How she found her way from Lahore to Blessed Redeemer in Bounds with a scant handful of English phrases remains a puzzle to me. I guess other relatives of Pakistani victims mapped it out for her; there must be a network by now. And I'm certain the airline helped out with travel arrangements and lodging.

But I knew so little beyond what I saw in front of me. She was very dark. A middle-aged woman—could have been anywhere in her forties or fifties. Her hands looked rough and callused, and she walked with a stoop; it was clear she hadn't had an easy life. She wore some sort of native dress: loose, flowing trousers with a dress over them; a long, gauzy scarf covered her hair much of the time, though, when it fell, she let it lie draped over her shoulders like an academic hood. She never varied from white—I came to see it as a color of mourning.

For the rest of the week, coming into the church at odd hours, making a reverence, I'd move quietly, wondering if she were present. I surprised her at her devotions only once more. To say that she was "kneeling" wouldn't be accurate: she was face to the floor. I noticed that the indentation—what looked like a dimple or pockmark—in the middle of her forehead came from pressing her brow to a tiny, figured piece of red clay she set on the ground in front of her. She had a rosary, too, of the same unbaked clay.

She visited with me twice more. It puzzled me how she

managed to get herself around in Bounds. Except for "thank you very much," her speech remained impenetrable to me, and I'm supposed to be a trained listener. I had to wander through a thicket of strange sounds before I caught a glimmer of the path—a single English word or a cluster of words I thought I recognized. It was the tone, if anything, that guided me.

She talked—I listened. Maybe she thought I understood. Maybe I did. She looked me in the eyes as though it were a real conversation and there were no question of my not understanding. Somewhere along into it, the lamentation began. This always happened. The particular words were beyond me, but I knew grieving when I heard it. I'd be sitting there facing her, nodding, or venturing a few consoling noises, waiting for the first tuck in the flow, the quaver, the breaking off from words. Then the tears—a language we all know. At the end, she'd wipe her eyes with the corner of her scarf and rise, making a perfunctory bow to me. I'd stand also and nod—a nod that might pass for a bow, if that were appropriate. I refrained from patting her shoulder or shaking her hand; I knew enough to assume that these gestures would be laden with other meanings for her. She thanked me in English again, that formula she'd mastered. I thanked her for her trust in me. I spoke slowly, summoning up three words for "trust" in hopes of her recognizing one of them. Each time she visited, we exchanged formal good-byes—I had no way of knowing which time would be the last.

Then she disappeared, leaving a photograph of her son on the table in the vestibule. We've got quite a little gallery there by now. From time to time, I wonder what it was that transpired between us. Something. What was it?

There were no impediments of language between myself and my most recent visitor, a young woman from Spokane, Washington. The woman wasn't related to any of the passengers on board, but she'd met a young man on the connecting flight from Spokane to San Diego and she'd been trying to trace him ever since. He'd been scheduled to board Flight 582 for the long leg back East.

"I'm looking for a close friend" was how she began. But when I asked her the logical next question, "Who might that be?" she confessed that she didn't know his last name. His first name was William, she was sure of that. He'd told her that he was studying economics at Yale. "I realize Yale is a big place," she said, "but when I phoned, they didn't even try and help me. They were quite rude, if you want to know."

"Tell me a little more about him," I suggested, already doubtful that it could be much.

"Well . . . he's twenty, very, very bright, and graduating this semester. This semester or next, I'm not real sure. He was going from Spokane—I think it was his cousin he'd been visiting there. Going from Spokane to San Diego by American Airlines. In San Diego, he changed over to Maxim for the flight east. Maxim wouldn't give me a copy of their passenger list for that flight. I tried every way I could think of to get my hands on it. Nothing doing. They said they were bound by law, one of those invasion of privacy things. I should've lied and told them I was his cousin or something. His name never came up in the newspaper listings—at least, none of the ones I read. I've never met anybody like him. He was so friendly—the nicest personality. I miss him so—"

I took out my master list. Together, we pored over the names of the injured and the dead. There was a young man listed, a certain John W. Stinnett from Bridgeport, Connecticut. That sounded close to me. The middle initial "W" very likely stood for William. Stinnett was twenty-one years old. Deceased. He sounded like the young man she was seeking, close enough in age and probable destination. The logical next step would be to determine whether John W. Stinnett joined Flight 582 after a connecting flight from Spokane. I offered to inquire for her.

"Oh, no"—she shook her head vehemently—"don't bother. But thanks. That couldn't be him, see, because he didn't have a middle name. We happened to discuss that. I mentioned that I'd always hated mine: it's Cynthia Prudence Washburn. I go by Cindy, just plain Cindy. It drives me crazy if anybody calls me by my middle name. He told me he never had any problems like that since he didn't have a middle name. So it couldn't be him."

I agreed to display the small handprinted poster she'd brought along with her, posting one on my office door, one in the parish hall, and one on the wall in the vestibule, on the bulletin board over the table with all the photographs and the visitors' sign-in book. It looked something like one of those WANTED notices you find tacked up on the bulletin boards in most post offices, WANTED and MOST WANTED that the F.B.I. puts out. Minus the mug shot, though.

I invited her to sign the visitors' book.

"Could I read it?"

"Sure," I said, "but it will take you a while."

I went back to my office while she had a go at it. When she was done, she came around to let me know that she was really leaving this time. "Any luck?" I asked. She didn't answer; one glance at her face and I knew there wasn't. I promised once again to let her know if I heard anything. "If I don't find him this way, I never will," she admitted. "He means so much to me." I think she realized then how slim her chances were. I escorted her to the front door and lingered there, watching her make her way down the street. At the corner, she waved once over her shoulder without looking back.

The visitors don't come in droves any longer and I don't always see the ones who come in and sign the book, or who stop by to light a candle or leave flowers. Sometimes they're hothouse flowers in expensive formal arrangements, but, more often these days, they're wildflowers gathered from the side of the road and mixed with what we tend to think of as weeds—copper mallow, henbit, senna, or mustard weed—telling us that outsiders have left them. The parish council may grumble over the mess but the circle widens.

The circle widens . . . On my way out, I always pause to read the latest entries in the visitors' book. There are two new ones. A woman from Kansas City, Missouri *(Pray for Robert)* is followed by a man from Syracuse, New York *(Just to look)*. The page is only one line short of full, so I turn it over and leave the book open for the next person coming in.

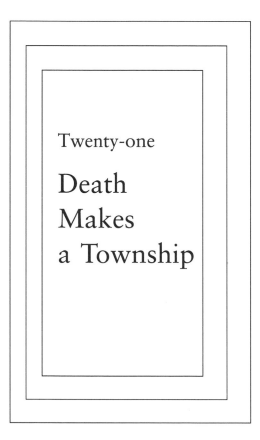

Twenty-one

Death Makes a Township

WE WERE PAST SPRING, by the books, but not really there yet. Given notice of arrival is all. It was up and down, bleary then fine, never knowing from one day to the next. Time of year I call "green-feed season." You could taste it in the milk—a green taste—dank, chill, a smidge oniony. The cows eating too much new grass, what it was, and it wasn't only the cows. If you'd happened along First Street to that new Allsups on the corner, you'd see a sign in the window:

Eggs from Happy Hens
on the ground, plenty of
Green Feed, with Rooster

And you'd notice "Green Feed" underlined twice.

But—about the cows—my friend Cloteal will take one short swallow of our new milk and say, "They've been eating flowers again." Now I doubt that altogether, flower-tastes being too pale to mention. What I taste is wild onion—and earth. Cloteal's a poetess and inclined to flower things up.

Me—I've always prided myself on being down to earth, what they call a "realist." Especially lately: I've been spring cleaning. I started out last week at the post office, then tackled the closets at home on the weekend. Today, it's been scrubbing windows and taking down the curtains to wash. Did two big washes and vacuumed all the rugs. I'm still struggling with mashed-in raisins and popcorn the kids spilled decades ago; dropped things keep on turning up.

The garage was next on my list. First off, stacking things in piles, finding out—*facing*—what I've squirreled away out of sight over the years. I made three piles: *Keep, Give or Sell, Dump,* then had to start up a fourth for *Undecided.* Of course, it was *Undecided* that got to be the biggest heap. Useless, vexing things with memories attached: there was the extra board for the big dining room table—the table I sold when I knew Al was gone for good, and the giant stew pot that grew too big for a household of one and sometimes a little company. There was a pole lamp minus the wiring, two folding lawn chairs needing to be rewove, and a heap of old plowshares. The plowshares I'd surely keep; they were Troy's first set.

I'd started cleaning well before seven in the morning, and hadn't stopped for lunch, so round about noon I decided enough was enough. It was one of those spur-of-the-moment things. I called Cloteal to see if she might want to join me, and she did. She wanted "something special," so we thought of K-Bob's near Hardesty.

My lucky day, it so happened. I'd never won anything in my life—until that lunch. It was the twenty-fifth anniversary of the restaurant and they were celebrating. We were sitting there, Cloteal and me, all decided on what we were going to order and nobody coming to take the order, when we heard a bell clanging. It was one of the waitresses and a fellow along with her carrying a milk pail, making the rounds of the tables, hailing, "A winner! A winner!" I caught the eye of the other waitress; she rushed past us, promising, "I'll be with you, just hold on." But she never came; it was the pair with the bell and the bucket who—after a little ceremony—finally took our orders. Turned out I was the winner they'd been making the ruckus about, their twenty-fifth customer since noon. They'd been coming to our table all along. So I drew a slip of paper from the pail and read it out loud as they asked me to. Said I'd won a chef salad for a dollar twenty-five, the 1968 price, but I had to claim my prize no later than the end of this month.

Doesn't sound like much, maybe, but it gave me a boost. I *did* feel lucky—and energetic—for hours afterwards. I returned to the garage and decided some of the

Undecided things, and gathered a big bundle of work clothes for the Bounds summer sale.

Near five, I decided to call it quits. It was still sunny, though I'd missed the best of it. I needed to be out in the air after all those dark corners and dust, so I set out for a stroll, my usual stroll down Memory Lane, which at my age happens to be the cemetery. Death makes a township, I thought, and for me there'll soon be more in it than outside it.

It's a pretty place, Bounds Cemetery. There's a white gate that stays shut most of the time, and a short stretch of picket fence on either side of that. The fence is mainly for decoration, because the place is wide-open on the other three sides, where a hardpan road sweeps around it. It's really one of the nicest spots in town with a well-established lawn, a few salt cedars, a little shinnery oak, and some—not too many—mesquite. Those things take over like weeds if you let them.

Thinking back to the days before the crash, I was filled with wonderment. Seemed like I'd lived in a fish tank till then, a fish tank full of sky. A sky bleary or bright or blowing, but never an unimagined thing. There were the drouths, the dust storms, the hail-outs, but, through it all, I remained in the fish tank, in Bounds, the walls hard and clear as glass. Then came the crash, and something shattered. Seemed like the whole world poured in . . .

I turned west by the Blackwelder family plot, the way I usually go. Six stones, Bruce was the last. Their plot always looks a bit unkempt—no Blackwelders left to tend it.

The Moseleys are neighbors to the Blackwelders. A strip of concrete—like a yard fence, but low—marks off the boundaries. Most of the Moseleys lived normal lifetimes, except for Ben—he never made it to twenty. Single vehicle accident. Most people know what that means. *Life is a voyage that's homeward bound* is what his stone says.

We hoped so. We surely did hope.

Crawleys next. They aren't the best-loved family in town. "Lots of little Crawleys in the ground," kids like to tease. For a fact, they don't live long.

There were a lot of little Crawleys there before me, and stacked up pretty close, cheek by jowl, hip by haunch. Not much in the way of summing up, not by words, anyway. Only their names scratched on a bit of concrete. Some not even that. A couple of them had figurines of china glass; a rooster was leaning against one stone that had only a pair of dates on it; the stone next to it, with a cocker spaniel that'd been broken and glued back together, had a name but no dates. Then there were the grown Crawleys, the brothers Rick and Birch: two concrete slabs stuck full of pebbles. Rick had fishing tackle set in the concrete for his —fishing was his favorite thing. Birch had spark plugs in his.

That set me to wondering what my favorite thing would be. It wasn't postage stamps, or embroidered pot lifters, or biscuits with cream gravy, though I liked all those things. Our pastor, Orville Stemm, put that very question to us last Sunday. Told us this story about a potter who made cremation urns in the shape of the departed's favorite thing. Young man, who doted on his motorcycle and perished when it crashed, got a motorcycle urn. Old man who liked to chew got a spittoon . . . I wasn't at all sure what my favorite thing would be. How to choose? I liked so many things. I'd only to think of all those precious odds and ends I'd squirreled away in the garage. There wouldn't be any one clear shape for the way my life had gone—I'd scattered it in this, that, the other thing, in loose threads, clutter, moments. In baking and visiting and writing letters—unanswered gestures often, but not useless, I don't think. I passed Francie Alred's folks, then Bill Saunders and Annie Parker, Chip's uncle and mother, with a pint-sized stone next to them for Stan Parker—Chip's long-ago twin. And, at last, a few stones after that, I'd arrived. Come to the place I'd been heading to all along.

It was Troy's spot; mine would be next to it. I visit often but try not to linger long. Be time enough, soon enough, for staying on. "Stopped by to say hello, Troy," I said to the air.

He was the only Troy, the only one of that name, I'd ever known. Nobody could say for sure why his mother chose it. Troy thought it was something she'd read in high school made a lasting impression. She couldn't recall what it was, though. My guess is, it wasn't what she read, so much as having to read it, that made the impression. Hannah Wooten was not a reading woman.

That's all there is to it: the name TROY WOOTEN and the dates. All it says. "Don't glorify it, Glenna," he made me promise, "don't ever try." I hadn't.

There was a little chill in the air, though the sun was still full and clear. The air shone so hard it stung.

"Hello and good-bye, Troy," I said. "I've been thinking about you, missing you, nearly every minute."

One more stop on my way out—it's a new grave, the soil's still heaped high over it. Nobody knows the name, and all that's written on the stone is the date of the crash and FLIGHT 582—A YOUNG MAN. He'd stowed away in the cargo compartment. I never thought a stowaway could happen on a plane. Apparently it does, but only rarely. Anyway—nobody knew, nobody came to claim him, so we decided he was meant to stay here with us in Bounds.

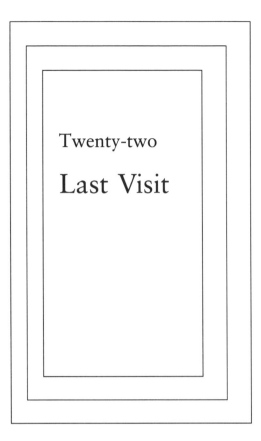

Twenty-two

Last Visit

I WENT BACK once more. That was last week, and nothing official. My paper had closed out the story some weeks before. Except for the results of the crash investigation, which wouldn't be announced for a long time, possibly years, and lawsuits, which might go on even longer, there was nothing further my editor felt our readers wanted to know about the crash or the town.

The big area story now was of a mixup in a sperm bank

in Dallas—light mischief with unforseeable consequences. The big national stories were on flooding in the Midwest and drive-by shootings in D.C.

By next week, or the next, we'd be tiring of these stories, too. But there was sure to be something else to take their place—a big financial swindle or a new sex scandal. Variety is what we're after. So why bother going back to anything? To Bounds? That's what I kept asking myself. I'd long since lost my bid on that power drill set in Hardesty—my reason for happening to be in the vicinity of Bounds on the day of the crash—and there was no other good reason to venture out this way. I simply wanted to see the field where the plane went down one last time. I guess I needed some final image to round off the story in my mind.

It was one of those shimmery days in May—a little windy. A single raft of clouds drifting across the blue. The night before, we'd had a good, long, *soaking* rain, the kind farmers pray for, and everything glistened green. That's one thing about a semi-arid region like this—growing things respond quickly, grateful for the least little bit of moisture—you can see the stems and leaves actually drinking it down.

The flatness I'd forgotten, the patience of it.

I drove right to the fence. The place was deserted, far as I could see. Unless you knew what had happened here, there was really nothing much to look at. The earth was starting to heal over. There were deep patches of weeds and, even in the barest spots, you could see a haze of green rising, some kind of leafy cover—what I'll call "prairie grass." I still don't know the names of the different kinds.

Something flickered in the sunlight, a scrap of metal glinting in the mass of clover at my feet, and I stooped to examine it. It could have been a fragment of an aluminum can, one of those pry-up lids. Or could have been something else—something the crash investigator and the dozers missed. For a moment, I thought of pocketing it, a sort of souvenir, but the moment passed and I let it lie.

Hard to believe this was a battlefield once, and not so long ago. Only the fence told you that this was no ordinary field, the faded wreaths one after another, lashed along the wire. Among them, I discovered something that wasn't there at the time I left. It was wired to one of the posts: a silvery windmill that kept on twirling, spooling out the light. Must have been in memory of some young child. It was the brightest thing around, whirling with a child's happy, restless energy.

The old woman who lives on the grounds—who owns the field, I should say—must have been spying on me from her window. Probably thought I was a trespasser, or one of the last of the mourners. I'd turned to simply glance at the house and, a minute later, she was cutting across the lawn, heading my way.

I introduced myself again. She insisted that she remembered me from the first night. Maybe so. She knew I was a reporter, though she couldn't recall what newspaper I was from.

We chatted for a while. I explained that I wasn't on assignment now, only wanting to see the place again, for myself. "You'd never guess what went on here," I said, "except for those"—pointing to the wreaths.

"Hard to believe, isn't it?" she said, her eyes roaming

beyond the fence. "The whole world has forgotten by now, but we're changed here in Bounds. We won't ever be the same."

"Changed how?" I wanted to know.

"It'll take some time to find out," she answered. "I feel it but don't know how to put words to it yet. We've come to realize—I have— Well, maybe, just this for now: how tangled together we are. All of us." She tried to say more —about all the people on earth who happen to be alive at the same time being alive together, connected together. Even the dead were not left out. "Like the leaves of the tree," she said, "the green and the fallen," and she raised her gnarled fingers to the light.

It made *some* sense, not a whole lot. First off, I don't think of the world as only one tree. A notion like that could only occur to someone living out in a place like this where trees are so scarce. Maybe I'm being overly literal, but I've seen too many trees competing to live, jostling for sunlight and air. Take any forest. Anyway—and I'm not being literal now—in the cities we tend to collide more than connect.

And, really, I wondered, what planet is she *on?* Disconnection, if anything, was the theme of the day. Pick anywhere you like: breakaway republics all over the globe, ethnic cleansing in Bosnia, Basque separatists in Spain . . . And look at the melting pot of the good old U.S. of A.—the races—the sexes, for that matter—all coming unglued—

But, then again, here were all these wreaths . . . from Bangkok, Atlanta, Dublin, Duluth . . . come together on a fence in Bounds. Here—in Bounds, Texas! Who could figure it?

She invited me up to the house for a cup of coffee. "Stay a little minute," she urged, but I knew it would be more like half an hour, so I thanked her, tapped my watch, and told her I'd have to be running along. "Some other time," I said. Before I set out, I'd thought about dropping in on the priest, but I didn't know whether he'd be in and, if he were, how long it would take to pick up our conversation from where we'd left off. So I decided to let that slide. It's only one story, I reminded myself; it's time to let go.

I took a last glance over the field. The cover was uneven, yet I felt certain it would green over in a month or two. By next growing season, she'd have a crop—wheat or sorghum, whatever it was she'd planned on. I wished her well. She shook my hand warmly and urged me to swing by again. I promised I would, knowing I probably wouldn't. I'd seen what I set out to see, and had a long road ahead.

Since leaving New York in 1983, A. G. Mojtabai has lived on the High Plains of Texas. Her understanding of this region and its ways informs *Called Out*, as well as her last two books, *Ordinary Time* and the nonfiction work *Blessed Assurance*, which won the Lillian Smith Award as the best book about the American South in 1986. The author has written four other novels, *Mundome, The 400 Eels of Sigmund Freud, A Stopping Place*, and *Autumn*, and has twice won awards from the American Academy of Arts and Letters: the Rosenthal Award in 1983, and an Academy Award in Literature in 1993.

A. G. Mojtabai has taught at Hunter College, New York University, and Harvard. Currently, she teaches at the University of Tulsa.